Libby and the Class Election

Shana Muldoon Zappa and Ahmet Zappa

with Zelda Rose

Bath • New York • Cologne • Melbourne • Delhi
Hong Kong • Shenzhen • Singapore

Libby and the
Class Election

This edition published by Parragon Books Ltd in 2016

Parragon Books Ltd
Chartist House
15–17 Trim Street
Bath BA1 1HA, UK
www.parragon.com

ISBN 978-1-4748-3736-1

Printed in UK

To our beautiful, sweet treasure,
Halo Violetta Zappa. You are pure light and joy
and our greatest inspiration. We love you soooo much.

May every step upon your path be blessed with positivity and
the understanding that you have the power within you to
manifest the most fulfilling life you can possibly imagine and
more. May you always remember that being different and true
to your highest self makes your inner star shine brighter.

Remember that you have the power of choice.... Choose thoughts
that feel good. Choose love and friendship that feed your spirit.
Choose actions for peace and nourishment. Choose boundaries
for the same. Choose what speaks to your creativity and unique
inner voice ... what truly makes you happy. And always know
that no matter what you choose, you are unconditionally loved.

Look up to the stars and know you are never alone.
When in doubt, go within ... the answers are all there.
Smiles light the world and laughter is the best medicine.
And NEVER EVER stop making wishes....

Glow for it....
Mummy and Daddy

And to everyone else here on "Wishworld":

May you realize that no matter where you are in life, no
matter what you look like or where you were born, you, too,
have the power within you to create the life of your dreams.
Through celebrating your own uniqueness, thinking positively,
and taking action, you can make your wishes come true.

Smile. The Star Darlings have your back.
We know how startastic you truly are.

Glow for it....
Your friends,
Shana and Ahmet

Starling Academy

NAME: Clover
BRIGHT DAY: 5 January
FAVOURITE COLOUR: Purple
INTERESTS: Music, painting, studying
WISH: To be the best songwriter and DJ on Starland
WHY CHOSEN: Clover has great self-discipline, patience and willpower. She is creative, responsible, dependable and extremely loyal.
WATCH OUT FOR: Clover can be hard to read and she is reserved with those she doesn't know. She's afraid to take risks and can be a wisecracker at times.
SCHOOL YEAR: Second
POWER CRYSTAL: Panthera
WISH PENDANT: Hair clip

* * * * * * * * * *

NAME: Adora
BRIGHT DAY: 14 February
FAVOURITE COLOUR: Sky blue
INTERESTS: Science, thinking about the future and how she can make it better
WISH: To be the top fashion designer on Starland
WHY CHOSEN: Adora is clever and popular and cares about the world around her. She's a deep thinker.
WATCH OUT FOR: Adora can have her head in the clouds and be thinking about other things.
SCHOOL YEAR: Third
POWER CRYSTAL: Azurica
WISH PENDANT: Watch

* * * * * * * * * *

NAME: Piper
BRIGHT DAY: 4 March
FAVOURITE COLOUR: Sea-foam green
INTERESTS: Composing poetry and writing in her dream journal
WISH: To become the best version of herself she can possibly be and to share that by writing books
WHY CHOSEN: Piper is giving, kind and sensitive. She is very intuitive and aware.
WATCH OUT FOR: Piper can be dreamy, absent-minded and wishy-washy. She can also be moody and easily swayed by the opinions of others.
SCHOOL YEAR: Second
POWER CRYSTAL: Dreamalite
WISH PENDANT: Bracelets

Student Reports

NAME: Astra
BRIGHT DAY: 9 April
FAVOURITE COLOUR: Red
INTERESTS: Individual sports
WISH: To be the best athlete on Starland — to win!
WHY CHOSEN: Astra is energetic, brave, clever and confident. She has boundless energy and is always direct and to the point.
WATCH OUT FOR: Astra is sometimes cocky, self-centred, condescending and brash.
SCHOOL YEAR: Second
POWER CRYSTAL: Quarrelite
WISH PENDANT: Wristbands

* * * *** * *** *** *

NAME: Tessa
BRIGHT DAY: 18 May
FAVOURITE COLOUR: Emerald green
INTERESTS: Food, flowers, love
WISH: To be successful enough so she can enjoy a life of luxury
WHY CHOSEN: Tessa is warm, charming, affectionate, trustworthy and dependable. She has incredible drive and commitment.
WATCH OUT FOR: Tessa does not like to be rushed. She can be quite stubborn and often says no. She does not deal well with change and is prone to exaggeration. She can be easily sidetracked.
SCHOOL YEAR: Third
POWER CRYSTAL: Gossamer
WISH PENDANT: Brooch

* * * *** * *** *** *

NAME: Gemma
BRIGHT DAY: 2 June
FAVOURITE COLOUR: Orange
INTERESTS: Sharing her thoughts about almost anything
WISH: To be valued for her opinions on everything
WHY CHOSEN: Gemma is friendly, easygoing, funny, extroverted and sociable. She knows a little bit about everything.
WATCH OUT FOR: Gemma talks — a lot — and can be a little too honest sometimes and offend others. She has a short attention span and can be superficial.
SCHOOL YEAR: First
POWER CRYSTAL: Scatterite
WISH PENDANT: Earrings

Starling Academy

NAME: Cassie

BRIGHT DAY: 6 July

FAVOURITE COLOUR: White

INTERESTS: Reading, crafting

WISH: To be more independent and confident, and less fearful

WHY CHOSEN: Cassie is extremely imaginative and artistic. She is a voracious reader and is loyal, caring and a good friend. She is very intuitive.

WATCH OUT FOR: Cassie can be distrustful, jealous, moody and brooding.

SCHOOL YEAR: First

POWER CRYSTAL: Lunalite

WISH PENDANT: Glasses

*** ** ** ⯈ ** ** **

NAME: Leona

BRIGHT DAY: 16 August

FAVOURITE COLOUR: Gold

INTERESTS: Acting, performing, dressing up

WISH: To be the most famous pop star on Starland

WHY CHOSEN: Leona is confident, hardworking, generous, open-minded, optimistic, caring and a strong leader.

WATCH OUT FOR: Leona can be vain, opinionated, selfish, bossy, dramatic and stubborn, and is prone to losing her temper.

SCHOOL YEAR: Third

POWER CRYSTAL: Glisten paw

WISH PENDANT: Cuff

*** ** ** ⯈ ** ** **

NAME: Vega

BRIGHT DAY: 1 September

FAVOURITE COLOUR: Blue

INTERESTS: Exercising, analysing, cleaning, solving puzzles

WISH: To be the top student at Starling Academy

WHY CHOSEN: Vega is reliable, observant, organized and focused.

WATCH OUT FOR: Vega can be opinionated about everything, and she can be fussy, uptight, critical, arrogant and easily embarrassed.

SCHOOL YEAR: Second

POWER CRYSTAL: Queezle

WISH PENDANT: Belt

Student Reports

NAME: Libby

BRIGHT DAY: 12 October

FAVOURITE COLOUR: Pink

INTERESTS: Helping others, interior design, art, dancing

WISH: To give everyone what they need — both on Starland and through wish granting on Wishworld

WHY CHOSEN: Libby is generous, articulate, gracious, diplomatic and kind.

WATCH OUT FOR: Libby can be indecisive and may try too hard to please everyone.

SCHOOL YEAR: First

POWER CRYSTAL: Charmelite

WISH PENDANT: Necklace

···📛·*··*··*

NAME: Scarlet

BRIGHT DAY: 3 November

FAVOURITE COLOUR: Black

INTERESTS: Crystal climbing (and other extreme sports), magic, thrill seeking

WISH: To live on Wishworld

WHY CHOSEN: Scarlet is confident, intense, passionate, magnetic, curious and very brave.

WATCH OUT FOR: Scarlet is a loner and can alienate others by being secretive, arrogant, stubborn and jealous.

SCHOOL YEAR: Third

POWER CRYSTAL: Ravenstone

WISH PENDANT: Boots

···📛·*··*··*

NAME: Sage

BRIGHT DAY: 1 December

FAVOURITE COLOUR: Lavender

INTERESTS: Travel, adventure, telling stories, nature and philosophy

WISH: To become the best Wish-Granter Starland has ever seen

WHY CHOSEN: Sage is honest, adventurous, curious, optimistic, friendly and relaxed.

WATCH OUT FOR: Sage has a quick temper! She can also be restless, irresponsible and too trusting of others' opinions. She may jump to conclusions.

SCHOOL YEAR: First

POWER CRYSTAL: Lavenderite

WISH PENDANT: Necklace

Introduction

You take a deep breath, about to blow out the candles on your birthday cake. Clutching a coin in your fist, you get ready to toss it into the dancing waters of a fountain. You stare at your little brother as you each hold the end of a dried wishbone, about to pull. But what do you do first?

You make a wish, of course!

Ever wonder what happens right after you make that wish? *Not much*, you may be thinking.

Well, you'd be wrong.

Because something quite unexpected happens next. Each and every wish that is made becomes a glowing Wish Orb, invisible to the human eye. This undetectable orb zips through the air and into the heavens, on a one-way trip to the brightest star in the sky – a magnificent place called Starland. Starland is inhabited by Starlings, who look a lot like you and me, except they have a sparkly glow to their skin, and glittery hair in unique colours. And they have one more thing: magical powers. The Starlings use these powers to make good wishes come true, for when good wishes are granted, it results in positive energy. And the Starlings of Starland need this energy to keep their world running.

In case you are wondering, there are three kinds of Wish Orbs:

1) GOOD WISH ORBS. These wishes are positive and helpful and come from the heart. They are pretty and sparkly and are nurtured in climate-controlled Wish-Houses. They bloom into fantastical glowing orbs. When the time is right, they are presented to the appropriate Starling for wish fulfilment.

2) BAD WISH ORBS. These are for selfish, mean-spirited or negative things. They don't

sparkle at all. They are immediately transported to a special containment centre, as they are very dangerous and must not be granted.

3) IMPOSSIBLE WISH ORBS. These wishes are for things like world peace, curing diseases and unattainable requests that simply can't be granted by Starlings. These sparkle with an almost impossibly bright light and are taken to a special area of the Wish-House with tinted windows to contain the glare they produce. The hope is that one day they can be turned into good wishes the Starlings can help grant.

Starlings take their wish granting very seriously. There is a special school, called Starling Academy, that accepts only the best and brightest young Starling girls. They study hard for four years, and when they graduate, they are ready to start travelling to Wishworld to help grant wishes. For as long as anyone can remember, only graduates of wish-granting schools have ever been allowed to travel to Wishworld. But things have changed in a very big way.

Read on for the rest of the story....

Prologue

TOP-SECRET HOLO-COMMUNICATION
(Warning: This memorandum will disappear
five seconds after it has been read.)

TO: The Star Darlings Guest Lecturers
    Professor Margaret Dumarre
    Professor Dolores Raye
    Professor Illumia Wickes
    Professor Elara Ursa

Professor Lucretia Delphinus

Professor Eugenia Bright

cc: Lady Cordial, Director of Admissions

FROM: Lady Stella, Headmistress

RE: Star Darlings Update

To All:

I am writing to inform you that Operation Star Darlings is up and running! My theory – that young Starlings granting the wishes of young Wishlings would result in a greater amount of wish energy – is correct.

However, I have both good and bad news. The good news is that the mission was successful and we collected a significant amount of wish energy. The bad news is there was a glitch in initial Wisher identification and the amount of wish energy that was collected was not quite as large as we had anticipated.

What have we learned from this? It is clear we must continue to diligently support and train our Star Darlings so that the remaining eleven missions go seamlessly and we will be able to collect the most wish energy possible.

When will the next mission happen and who will be chosen? Only time will tell. But I am cautiously optimistic that Operation Star Darlings will be a success.

Thank you for your help and your discretion.

Starfully yours,
Lady Stella

CHAPTER
1

The first thing Libby noticed when she blinked awake was the delightful scent that permeated her dorm room. She sat up in bed and inhaled the perfumed air.

"Smells amazing, doesn't it?" asked Gemma.

Libby looked over at her roommate lying in bed across the room. Gemma's bright orange hair, messy from sleep, formed a wild halo around her head as she lay there, sniffing deeply. The two girls turned their attention to the vase of coral-coloured flowers that had been waiting for them in their dorm room when they returned from dinner the evening before.

"I still can't figure out what kind of flowers they are," said Libby. "I don't recognize them, but they smell just like blushbelles." Blushbelles were her favourite flower. They were pink, released puffs of sparkling stardust, and had a sweetly spicy scent that she thought was simply the loveliest smell on all of Starland.

"Blushbelles?" Gemma snorted. "What are you talking about?" she said. "It smells like orange-and-vanilla ice pops – just like chatterbursts. I can't believe we're even having this conversation!" She gave Libby a quizzical look.

Libby liked to keep the peace. She usually carefully weighed her words before she spoke. But for some reason, she sat up in bed and heard herself say, rather forcefully, in fact, "You're crazy."

Gemma blinked in surprise. "No, *you're* crazy," she retorted. "You're as crazy as a bloombug." Libby gave her roommate an annoyed look. Bloombugs were small purple-and-pink spotted bugs that went wild every time there was a full moon during the warmer months of the Time of Lumiere, hopping up and down and squealing with delight at the warmer weather and longer daylight hours the season brought. Gemma sniffed. "Well, no matter how crazy you are, you have to admit that this is the sweetest thing you've ever...."

Her voice trailed off as she noticed that Libby had pulled her soft pink blanket over her head, obviously ignoring her. Gemma threw back the covers and nimbly hopped out of bed. She opened her wardrobe and grabbed her bathrobe. "I call first stars on the sparkle shower!" she cried.

Libby sighed. Gemma had called first stars on the sparkle shower every day that week. They were supposed to take turns. She removed the covers and took a deep, calming breath. Then another for good measure. She smiled, feeling much better. There. No reason to get annoyed. She and Gemma were the perfect roommates, the envy of all the other Star Darlings. They got along well, accepting each other's idiosyncrasies, easily working through any issues that came up, and never letting resentments get in the way of their respect and affection for each other. Sure, Gemma had an impulsive personality, and Libby sometimes had difficulty making even the smallest decision without carefully weighing the pros and cons (deciding what to order for dinner sometimes required the thought process others reserved for major life decisions). But they had similar live-and-let-live personalities that served them both well. So it really confused Libby that she was feeling irked that morning. And over something as silly as a vase of flowers that would probably have wilted by the afternoon!

Libby yawned and stretched. She slipped her feet into a pair of fluffy pink slippers and shuffled towards the mysterious bouquet of flowers, which was sitting on her pink desk, exactly where the two roommates had discovered it the night before to their delight and surprise.

She leaned over and took a deep sniff. She shook her head. The smell was actually more spicy than sweet in her estimation. Just like blushbelles, no question about it. Maybe Gemma was teasing her. She sighed with happiness as she surveyed her half of the double room. She, like all incoming students at Starling Academy, had filled out an extensive questionnaire about her dorm-room preferences. The results were spectacular. Her half of the room was pink, pink, and more pink as far as the eye could see, just as she had requested, from the round bed, with its padded fabric headboard, to the sumptuous rug, recessed wall lights, desk/dressing table, and sparkling crystal chandelier. (The lovely white lacquered dresser with spindly legs that stood in the corner was the sole non-pink touch.) And the wide, low pink table was surrounded by luxurious floor cushions. It was the perfect place for friends to gather, and Libby often invited her classmates over to hang out during their free time.

Luckily, Gemma was very social and fun-loving, too. But on the occasional day that she wasn't in the mood for company, she would just draw the starry curtain that ran along the middle of the room, climb into bed and read or listen to music. But she could usually be coaxed to join in when the conversation got too good to ignore.

Gemma stepped into the room. Her skin glimmered, covered in a fresh layer of sparkles from her shower. Star Darlings were born with glittery skin and hair, but a daily sparkle shower helped keep them as luminous as possible. Libby headed in next, and the sparkle shower, invigorating and refreshing, cleared her mind and improved her mood. She applied her toothlight, first to the top row, then to the bottom. Starlings used their toothlights twice a day, in the morning and the evening, to keep their teeth as clean, white and sparkly as could be.

Libby put her toothlight back in the mirrored cabinet, closed it and stared at her reflection for a moment, taking in her long pink hair, alabaster skin, rose-coloured eyes and dimpled chin. She smiled at her reflection and headed back into the other room. She found Gemma sitting on her bed, tying her yellow shoelaces. She had put on an orange mesh three-quarter-length-sleeved shirt over an orange tank top and matching capri pants and pulled her hair into two cute pigtails.

She looked effortlessly hip, as always. As soon as she spotted Libby, she launched right back into the conversation, as though no time had passed. "So wouldn't you agree that they are the most delicious-smelling flowers ever? I mean, I have never smelled anything so sweet in my entire life. No lie. Have you?"

Libby had indeed smelled something sweeter. For her sixth birthday, her parents had taken her and eleven of her closest friends on a behind-the-scenes private tour of the Floffenhoofer Candy Factory. The very air in the jellyjooble processing room had nearly knocked her over with its fruity deliciousness. Just thinking about it made her mouth water. "Well, once I went on a –"

"Come to think of it, we had an orchard of goldenella trees on the farm," Gemma continued, as if she had never asked Libby her opinion. "You know, the kind that bloom non-stop for one week straight, and the flowers pop off the tree just like popcorn. When they bloomed, Tessa and I would just drop to the ground and roll around in the flowers. The smell was intoxicating! They positively carpeted the grass." She shook her head. "But even that was nothing like this delicious fragrance." She sniffed again.

"Well, I once –" Libby tried again.

"And when I say carpet of flowers, I'm talking

wall-to-wall," Gemma pressed on. "Nothing but lemon-yellow blossoms as far as the eye could see. And they didn't fade at all. It looked like a sea of sunshine. I remember one time when Tessa and I decided to...."

Libby, who usually listened with pleasure to Gemma's stories, found herself tuning out. Gemma's older sister, Tessa, was a third-year student and also a Star Darling. The sisters had been raised on a farm far out in the countryside, in a place called Solar Springs. There wasn't even a real town nearby, Gemma had told her, just a dusty old general store, where they did their very occasional shopping. They grew nearly everything they needed on the farm. Libby, who'd had a completely different upbringing in Starland City, had heard countless stories about their life and thoroughly enjoyed each one. It was such a different existence from hers, and she found it fascinating. And Gemma loved to talk about it. She liked to talk in general, actually. When she was in the mood, she could talk all day long, from the moment she woke up to when she went to bed. Libby had even been woken up in the middle of the night by Gemma talking in her sleep! But Libby had just laughed and gone back to bed. Libby loved a good discussion and a friendly argument.

But for some reason she was not enjoying it that day.

Libby finished getting dressed in a pink dress with star-shaped pockets and white tights embroidered with pink stars. She hung her Wish Pendant, a necklace that resembled a constellation of golden stars, around her neck and fastened the clasp. Her signature look was sweetly stylish. She stood in front of the mirror in her wardrobe, brushing her long pink hair. The exact shade of candyfloss and jellyjoobles, it rippled down her back. Her silky, flowing rosy-hued hair was her secret pride.

"So who do you think sent us the flowers?" Gemma asked. "There wasn't a holo-card. Why would anyone be so mysterious? If you're sending such a nice gift, you'd think you'd want to get credit for it. That reminds me of the time I –"

"That's a good question," interrupted Libby. She sifted through the evidence. Neither of them recognized the glittery flowers, so they must be rare (and, most likely, expensive). Receiving them had been a pleasant, unexpected surprise. And anything rare, beautiful, thoughtful or extravagant in Libby's life always came from one place. "My parents must have sent them," she said with a smile. "They love surprises." *Especially expensive ones,* she thought.

Gemma, who was the secondary beneficiary of many a care package from Libby's parents, Erica and Miles, nodded. "Hey! I think you're right!" she exclaimed.

As if on cue, Libby's holo-phone rang and an image of her mother, drumming her fingers impatiently on the Starcar's dashboard, was projected in the air. She hesitated because she wasn't sure she felt like talking to her mum at the moment, but she accepted the call with a swipe of her hand.

"Sweetheart!" said her mother, appearing as a live hologram in front of Libby. She was sitting next to Libby's father on their way to work. Libby's parents worked hard as investment bankers at a large firm and liked to enjoy the best life had to offer, showering their daughter with pricey gifts and one-of-a-kind experiences. Of course these rare fragrant blooms had come from them!

"Hi, Mum. Hi, Dad!" said Libby.

Gemma popped her head into the frame. "Hi, there!" she shouted.

Libby's dad put down his holo-reader and smiled. "Hello, girls. How's school?" he asked.

"Fine," said Libby, not looking at Gemma. It was a weird feeling not to be able to share everything that was going on at school with her mum and dad. But the Star Darlings had to keep their new duties top secret, even from their parents. Libby changed the subject quickly. "So we got the flowers you sent. They're beautiful. Thanks a lot."

"Yeah, thank you!" Gemma called out. "We love them."

Libby's mum looked confused. "Flowers? We didn't send you any flowers," she said. She turned to her husband. "Miles, we should have sent the girls flowers! That's such a nice idea!"

"Well, how about some glimmerchips?" offered Libby's dad. "We could send you a case or two."

"Yes, please," said Gemma automatically. She had never tasted the thin, crispy, salty and, yes, glimmery chips before she had started at Starling Academy, and she had developed quite a taste for them.

Libby shook her head. "We're fine, Daddy." She still had an unopened case under her bed. "But thank you."

"Starsweetie, the actual reason I called, besides to say hello, is to discuss your upcoming mid-Time of Shadows break," Libby's mother explained, pulling up a holo-calendar in the air in front of her. Libby could see that it was already packed with events and plans. Her parents always had a very full social calendar. "Daddy and I were thinking we'd go to Supernova Island. Or maybe Glamora-ora," she said, naming two exclusive holiday destinations. The holidays were still a way off, but Libby's parents were so busy they had to schedule everything months in advance.

Gemma's eyes were wide. "Wow," she mouthed, stunned into uncustomary silence. Her parents didn't like to leave the farm for more than a couple of hours at a time, so the sisters always spent their holidays at home.

Libby twirled a piece of her pink hair around her finger, a grimace on her face. She hated disappointing her parents. This wasn't going to be easy.

"That's not an attractive look, my dear," said her mother. "Is something wrong?"

"I ... uh ... was talking to Aunt Kit about joining her on a volunteering holiday during break," Libby explained. "We're thinking of travelling from city to city, helping out at different orphanages and animal shelters. And I might even be able to get some credits for school." Aunt Kit and Libby's mum were sisters, but they couldn't have been more different. Libby adored her mother, but she had so much more in common with the young, altruistic Kit, who loved helping others even more than she enjoyed travelling – which was saying a lot.

The matching looks of dismay on her parents' faces would have been funny if they hadn't been so disconcerting to Libby. It was painful for her to disappoint anyone, particularly her generous and kind parents. But you'd think she had told them she wanted them to take her camping on the Isle of Misera, a barren, rocky, uninhabitable island off the coast of New Prism. Libby sighed. The problem was that her parents just didn't get her.

Until Libby was ten years old, she had been unaware that she lived an exceptional life. She hadn't given a second thought to any of it – the huge sprawling mansion in the fanciest neighbourhood in Starland City, Starland's largest metropolis; the exclusive holidays; the wardrobeful of expensive clothes and shoes and accessories; any toy she desired, plus many more she hadn't even realized she had wanted until she received them. All that changed one day when she was off from school. The family's housekeeper was away, so little Libby's parents took her to work with them. She was playing in the conference room with her newest toy, an exclusive child-sized doll that could have full conversations on any subject with its owner, when a little girl walked in. She was the daughter of the building's caretaker and she was totally fascinated with Libby's doll. When Libby asked the girl if she had one just like it at home, she was shocked to hear that the girl didn't own a doll of any kind. Libby was dubious. Was that even possible? The girl explained that her parents didn't have money for unnecessary things. Libby felt terrible. "Take it, it's yours," she said to the girl. The look of pure joy on the girl's face staggered Libby. The feeling she got from giving was much better than the happiness she got from receiving. She went home that night and took a good look around her. Meeting the girl had really opened her eyes to her privileged existence and the joy she could bring others with her generosity.

Libby had started small, donating the toys she didn't play with to a children's hospital. Her parents were amused, calling her "our little philanthropist". But when Libby gave away every other toy she owned, and then asked for donations to her favourite charity instead of gifts on her Bright Day, they began to object. They especially did not appreciate it when she questioned their lavish lifestyle, which they felt they deserved, as they had earned it through their hard work.

Libby's mother spoke first. "That's our Libby, always thinking about others," she said. Libby perked up. Maybe they were starting to see her point of view....

"And never about us!" her parents said together.

No such luck. Libby felt her spirits deflate like a punctured floating star globe.

"The choice is yours, my love," said her father sadly. "But we were looking forward to spending some quality time relaxing together, like we always do on holiday."

Libby was careful not to smile, as she could recall many family holidays when she had been left to her own devices while her parents took their daily holo-conference calls. Her parents didn't really know how to relax.

"Well, we've arrived," announced Libby's dad in the fake cheerful voice Libby knew all too well. The car would drop them off at the building's entrance, then park itself in their designated parking space.

"Bye, Mum and Dad, talk soon," said Libby, rushing off the phone. She was glad to be out of the starlight, but she still felt a lump in her throat as her parents signed off, about to begin another day of acquisitions and mergers. Or whatever it was they did all day.

She stood there for a moment. She was glad that Gemma understood that she needed a moment to collect her....

"Well," said Gemma. "That didn't go over so well. What are you going to do? Me, I guess I would just go to –"

Libby whirled around to face her roommate, about to give her a piece of her mind.

Just then, there was a knock at the door.

CHAPTER
2

Eager to work on their energy-manipulation skills, both girls tried to open the door at the same time, using their powers of concentration. This resulted in a standoff, since neither was particularly good at it yet. The door slid open an inch, then closed, then repeated the same motion several times. The visitor knocked again, louder. "Let me in!" a voice called out impatiently.

Finally, Libby backed off and allowed Gemma to do the honours. Gemma concentrated with all her might, her face turning quite red with the effort. The door slid open haltingly, and their visitor stepped inside.

It was Scarlet. "You guys might want to think about working on your energy-manipulation a bit more," she said. As a third-year student, she had more practice with it and was much better than they were.

"Oh, hey, Scarlet," Gemma said casually. But Libby could tell that her roommate was a little nervous. Libby couldn't blame her: Scarlet, with her intense punk-rock look and matching attitude, was pretty intimidating. She could be stand-offish, intense and mysterious – so much so that Libby had gone out of her way to avoid her at the beginning of the school year. But then, one day, feeling blue, she had curled up in the Illumination Library to read one of her favourite holo-books from childhood and looked up to discover that both she and Scarlet were deeply engrossed in *The Starling's Surprise*. They'd had a good laugh about it, then bonded over the common bout of homesickness that had led to the book selection. (Scarlet had sworn Libby to secrecy; she had a reputation to uphold!) Libby had realized that when you got to know her, Scarlet could also be kind and fun. But Gemma was not yet convinced. "Whatever you say," Gemma had said when Libby tried to explain it to her. "But until she's kind and nice to *me*, I just won't believe it." The rest of the Star Darlings, especially Leona, Scarlet's roommate, all seemed to feel the same way.

"Hey, I thought I'd stop by to see if you wanted to walk to the Celestial Café together," Scarlet said. She looked around her. "I forgot how nice your room is," she said. "It kind of reminds me of a beautiful sunset."

Gemma smiled despite herself. Libby looked at the room as if through Scarlet's eyes. The girl was right. The lighting – soft pink on Libby's side and cheerful orange on Gemma's – combined in the middle of the room to create a rosy glow that was warm and cosy. The two girls definitely had different tastes, but their furnishings fitted together nicely. Libby was a bit neater, her bed always made and her belongings stowed away. Gemma had a lot of stuff for her many interests – musical instruments, holo-books on almost every subject you could think of, stuffed animals, crafting supplies, flora she had collected on nature hikes, a variety of sporting equipment – and it was all crammed onto her floor-to-ceiling shelves.

The other Star Darlings' rooms were not quite so harmonious. Sage and Cassie, also first-year students, had a room that was a study in complete opposites – one side austere and the other quite cluttered. The room that second-years Piper and Vega shared was neat as a pin, in soothing shades of blue and green, but the similarity ended there. Piper's side was soft and dreamy, with soothing curved surfaces, lots of pillows and stacks of dream journals, while Vega's felt angular, clean and precise. Clover and Astra's room was a jarring combination of sporty and sleek. And over in the Big Dipper Dorm, Tessa and Adora's jumbled room reflected their duelling interests in science experiments and cooking. You never wanted to pick up a glass that wasn't handed specifically to you: it could be a tasty smoothie, but there was an equal chance that it could be a putrid-tasting potion nobody in her right mind would want to ingest.

And then there were Scarlet and Leona. Their room was as discordant as their relationship. Leona was as bright, flashy and in your face as her side of the room, with its warm golden glow, stage for impromptu shows and desk shaped like a dressing table surrounded by bright lightbulbs. Scarlet's space was designed so she could skateboard down its walls. It was certainly an interesting room. But Libby didn't feel truly comfortable there. Too much tension between the two roommates, maybe.

"Hey!" said Scarlet, spotting the bouquet. "You got those flowers, too! And so did Tessa and Adora, down the hall from me. They must be from Lady Stella, don't you think?" She took a deep sniff. "Aren't they amazing? They smell just like punkypows."

Libby and Gemma stared at each other. Now that was very odd!

Scarlet sat down on Libby's pristine pink bedding. "So when I came out of the sparkle shower this morning, what do you think I found?"

"A hungry glion, eating your flowers," offered Gemma. Libby knew her roommate was trying to be funny, but nobody laughed.

Scarlet gave Gemma her patented disdainful look, and Gemma, embarrassed, immediately busied herself with her Star-Zap.

"Nooo...." Scarlet drew the word out scornfully. "I found my roommate wearing my grandfather's top hat, that's what," she said. "Again! And again I told her to keep her hands off it. I remind her all the time that it's special, not to be worn, ever, and as usual she just ignores me."

She scowled. Before Scarlet's grandfather had completed his Cycle of Life, he had been the greatest and most famous magician Starland had ever known. He had been known as Preston the Prestidigitator, and Starlings had come from near and far to watch him perform. Preston had left his granddaughter his top hat, which Scarlet kept in a glass case, as if it was in a museum. Rumour had it that the end of his life cycle had been staged and that as part of an elaborate trick he would reappear on his next Bright Day. But Libby was too intimidated to ask Scarlet if it was true.

Scarlet shook her head. "You guys are so lucky, you get along so perfectly. What's your secret?"

Libby bristled and heard herself say, "We take turns deciding who gets to take the first sparkle shower in the morning."

Gemma narrowed her eyes at Libby. "We always listen to each other," she said.

Scarlet didn't notice the tension between the two girls. "Well, that's great," she said. "In any event, I'm hungry. Time for breakfast?"

The Star Darlings tended to sit together in the Celestial Café, at a table by the window overlooking the majestic Crystal Mountains. Libby always tried to grab a seat facing the view. Although Libby was friendly with many of the regular students, she had discovered that it was just easier to spend most of her time with her fellow Star Darlings. You could never let your guard down around the others, in case you accidentally let some top-secret information slip. Libby plopped herself down on the seat next to Gemma's sister, Tessa. Scarlet sat on Libby's other side and Gemma sat across from her, next to Tessa's roommate, Adora.

Tessa turned to them with a grin. "I just ordered the zoomberry pancakes," she said. "You should get them, too!"

"Whatever," said Gemma dismissively. "You know they're never as good as the ones Dad makes on the farm."

"I know," Tessa told her sister sympathetically. "The zoomberries aren't as fresh. But try them – they're still pretty good."

Adora, who sat across from Tessa, rolled her eyes. "Do you think I could sit through just one meal without hearing about how much better everything is on the farm?"

Tessa gave her roommate a hurt look.

Libby was surprised to hear Adora's words. She was usually so calm and collected.

The sisters looked at each other and shrugged. It was nearly impossible to ask the chatty sisters to stop talking about a subject that interested them. And farm-fresh food was one of their favourite subjects.

"May I take your order?" asked the Bot-Bot waiter, hovering by Gemma's shoulder.

"Hmmm," she mused. "I'm not sure what I'm in the mood for."

"I really think you'll like the starcakes, sis," said Tessa. "And you know how important breakfast is."

"It's the most important meal of the day," Gemma and Tessa said together. They laughed. "You sound like Mum!" they also said in unison.

"I was considering tinsel toast with bitterball preserves," Gemma said after a moment.

Tessa made a face. "I'm not sure if they put in enough sweetener," she said. "You know how sour it can be if it's not made correctly. I'd just go with the pancakes."

Gemma frowned. "Or how about a bowl of –"

"Enough!" said Adora. "Just order something. It's not a life-or-death decision. It's just food, for goodness' sake!"

Tessa looked puzzled. "Just food?" she said. "Who thinks that?"

Libby watched as Adora stood, walked to the other end of the table and sat down. Libby was surprised by her unusual behaviour. The two sisters didn't even seem to notice. Or maybe they just didn't care.

Scarlet nudged her with an elbow. "I don't think I've ever seen Adora act like that before," she said. "She's always so calm."

"Me neither," said Libby.

"Perhaps I could take your order now?" repeated the Bot-Bot waiter politely.

Libby decided to order since Gemma was still deliberating. "I ... um ... oh ... I guess I'll have the zoomberry starcakes," Libby said. "And a glass of Zing."

"Me too," said Scarlet.

"And I'll have the tinsel toast," Gemma said.

Tessa shook her head. "That's not going to be enough," she scolded. "Maybe you'd like a bowl of starberries and cream on the side?" she suggested.

"It's only going to remind me of Dad's starberry pie!" said Gemma.

Tessa nodded in sympathy. "You're right! Dad's starberry pie with a scoop of lolofruit ice cream," she said dreamily.

"Mmmmmmmm," said the sisters in unison.

Scarlet looked at Libby and raised her eyebrows. This was going to be one long meal....

CHAPTER
3

Sage squirmed in her seat. Libby, who was sitting right behind her, felt really sorry for her classmate. This couldn't be easy. Especially since they were in their final class after a long day of school – the Star Darlings' daily private lesson. And also because that day their guest lecturer was Professor Eugenia Bright, who taught Intro to Wish Fulfilment. Professor Eugenia Bright was tall and slender, with cropped turquoise hair and matching eyes. She was the most popular teacher on campus. There was always a long line of students outside her door during her office hours, looking for extra-credit assignments, wanting to make a good impression on the brilliant teacher, or simply seeking to bask in the warm glow of her presence.

Libby knew that Sage had to be completely miserable.

"So please explain to the class exactly what happened at the start of your mission," Professor Eugenia Bright said. "It will be most helpful for everyone to determine exactly when and how things took a turn."

Sage twisted the end of one of her thick purple plaits between her fingers. Noticing this, the teacher added more gently, "I'm sorry to make you uncomfortable, my dear. It's just that the other students can learn from your mis–" She stopped herself. "I mean, the *challenges* you faced on your mission."

Sage took a deep breath, then began to explain that she had arrived on Wishworld and headed to the school as directed by her Star-Zap. Using her powers of suggestion, she was able to convince the faculty and teachers that she belonged there and then she employed her observational skills to get clues as to whom the Wisher could be. After receiving information about a girl in a difficult situation, Sage had realized it seemed promising. So she headed over to talk with her and, after they had chatted for a while, discovered her wish.

"And what kind of wish was it?" the teacher asked.

"Well, it seemed like a good wish," Sage said slowly. "She was the new girl at school, and her mother, who was trying to help her make friends, had invited her classmates to her birthday party, against her wishes. But it was a big mistake. No one RSVP'd. She was embarrassed and upset that no one was going, and she wished that someone would come to her party."

The teacher nodded. "And what did you –"

Just then, there was a knock at the door. Sage exhaled loudly, glad for a brief break from the questioning.

"Class?" said Professor Eugenia Bright, indicating that one of them should use her energy-manipulation skills to open the door.

Sage brightened and took the opportunity to show off her formidable powers. The door slid open effortlessly. "Ooooooh," said the class in unison. Sage gave a smile. It was a small victory, but it was obvious it meant a lot to her at that moment.

There stood Lady Cordial, the head of admissions. The short, stocky woman, her purple hair cut in an unfortunate style that did not suit her face, had a pained expression. Leona said that she always looked like she had just broken your favourite vase and was trying to figure out how to tell you about it. Lady Cordial's eyes widened with surprise when she saw that the classroom was filled with students. "Oh, I'm s-s-s-sorry," she stuttered. "I didn't realize that class was still in s-s-s-session. I wanted to ask you a question about the admissions committee, but...." Her voice trailed off, and she stood in the doorway uncertainly.

"Well, hello there, Lady Cordial," Professor Eugenia Bright said kindly. She walked to the front of the room. "Always a pleasure to see you. Come right in. We can talk when class is dismissed." She thought for a moment. "Why don't you stay and observe our class until then?"

"Oh, what a st-st-startastic idea," cried Lady Cordial. She stepped inside, then somehow got her foot caught in her long purple skirt. She lunged forward, off balance, and grabbed the edge of the desk to catch herself, managing to knock over a plant sitting on it. Sparkly dirt spilled everywhere.

"Oh, my stars!" Lady Cordial said, her hands fluttering to her face in dismay.

Libby cringed. Poor Lady Cordial. She was so very clumsy.

There was a snort as one of the Star Darlings tried to hold in her laughter. Libby glanced up to see that Leona's face was bright red and her shoulders were shaking. Lady Cordial stared at the floor in embarrassment, her cheeks flushed, as she walked past the students to the back of the room. She sat at an empty desk, fortunately without further mishap. The dirt vanished almost immediately.

"We were discussing Sage's mission and the challenges she faced," Professor Eugenia Bright explained to Lady Cordial. "By identifying where her mission took a wrong turn, the other students may be able to learn from it." Libby saw Sage's shoulders sag once more.

Professor Eugenia Bright frowned. "So, where were we, class?" she asked.

Adora raised her hand. "Sage was just telling us that she had identified a Wishling who wanted some classmates to attend her birthday party."

The professor nodded. "And that certainly does sound like a worthy wish," she said. "But something seems off to me in the order of events. Can anyone guess what it is?"

Eleven hands shot up, including Libby's. Libby caught Sage giving her roommate, Cassie, a baleful look. But the tiny pale girl in the star-shaped glasses ignored Sage, her hand held straight up in the air.

"Yes, Astra?" said the teacher.

"You always need to verify the Wisher before trying to determine the wish," she answered. "Because if it isn't the right Wishling, then it doesn't matter what the wish is."

"Correct!" said Professor Eugenia Bright. "Now, Sage, did you help make this wish come true?"

"Yes," said Sage in a low voice. Her eyes were fixed on her desk.

"And what happened when it was granted?"

"Nothing," said Sage.

"No glorious burst of light and colour?" the professor asked.

"No," said Sage.

"No jolt as your Wish Pendant absorbed the wave of positive energy?"

Sage shook her head.

"Not even a tiny energy surge?" the teacher pressed.

"No," said Sage softly. She looked as if she might burst into tears.

"Exactly!" said the teacher. "No matter how worthy a wish is, if it hasn't been made by the correct Wishling, you will not be able to collect any wish energy," she said, clapping her hands together in time to her words to emphasize their importance. "In fact, you probably used a lot of your wish energy reserves in the pursuit of the wrong wish."

Sage nodded miserably.

"And the result was that you didn't collect as much wish energy as you could have."

Sage looked stricken. "I – I didn't? Lady Stella never told me that."

Professor Eugenia Bright bit her lip. "Oh," she said. She glided to the front of the room, where she walked back and forth, her hands clasped behind her back. She somehow managed to make something as commonplace as pacing look elegant and regal. "Now, did you try to confirm that you had identified the correct Wishling by looking at your Wish Pendant? Did it light up?"

Sage nodded, grimacing. "It did light up. But...."

Libby and the entire class leaned forward in anticipation. Professor Eugenia Bright and Lady Cordial did, too.

"But what?" the teacher prodded.

Sage sighed. "It was terrible. I didn't realize that as I was talking to the first Wishling, there was a second Wishling passing by right behind me. I stepped back and bumped into her. When I looked at my Wish Pendant for confirmation on the first Wishling...."

Professor Eugenia Bright held up a hand for Sage to stop talking. "Can anyone explain what happened here?" she asked. Again, eleven hands shot up in the air.

The teacher pointed to Vega.

"Sage thought that the birthday girl had made the wish she had been sent down to help grant, but it was actually the other Wishling. It's a classic case of Wisher misidentification," Vega explained. "I did some research on it in the library, and it happens more often than you would think. Historically, fifty per cent of Wish Missions are failures, and the main causes are either the Wisher or the wish being misidentified."

"That is correct, Vega," said Professor Eugenia Bright. "And starkudos for your extra work."

Vega sat back in her seat, looking very satisfied with herself.

Sage cleared her throat. "That's exactly what happened. I think I was so excited when I thought I had found the Wisher so quickly that I overlooked any other options."

The teacher nodded, laying a hand on Sage's shoulder. "You were in a very confusing situation. Luckily, you were able to realize your mistake, find the correct Wishling, identify her wish and collect energy."

Sage nodded. "Just not as much as I could have," she said with a sigh. She looked so miserable Libby felt the urge to help make her feel better. She raised her hand.

"Yes, Libby?" said Professor Eugenia Bright.

"I just wanted to say that it couldn't have been easy to go on the first mission. Sage was very brave.

And I think that complications are going to be unavoidable. This is all new to us. Sage taught us a lesson – that you have to make sure that no other Wishlings are around when you first verify your Wisher, just in case. And that's really helpful for all of us to know."

"Excellent point, Libby," said Professor Eugenia Bright. "I appreciate your ability to see both sides of the situation." She smiled at everyone. "Great work today, Starlings. Class dismissed."

Before Libby could stand up, Sage turned around and grabbed her hand. "Star salutations for what you said," Sage said to her. "It isn't easy being in the starlight."

Libby nodded. "I know," she said, patting Sage's shoulder. "And you're welcome." She stood up and straightened the skirt of her pink dress.

"Hold it, hold it!" cried a familiar voice. Libby turned around to see Leona climbing up onto a chair, her arms in the air. "I have an announcement to make. I'm starting a Star Darlings band, and I want you all to try out! I just ask one thing – please keep it quiet so everyone in school doesn't show up!"

Scarlet laughed. "As if!" she said.

Leona stuck out her tongue at her roommate.

"We just want to keep it small so it will be laid-back and fun, just like me! Let's meet in Star Quad at the band shell. Bring your instruments and come ready to rock out!"

"What about singers?" Gemma asked.

Leona threw back her head and laughed. "We've already got a lead singer – me! Every other instrument is up for grabs."

Scarlet rolled her eyes. But Libby started thinking.

As the Star Darlings filed out of the classroom and joined the throngs of students in the hallway eager to enjoy the precious few hours before dinnertime, Libby noticed a few girls staring at them and whispering. So did Leona. "Take a holo-picture," she told them huffily. "It lasts longer."

The girls gave her scornful looks but hurried away. Libby hid a smile. In order to keep their Star Darlings status secret from the rest of the school, they all had to pretend that they were in a special study group during last period. That bothered some Star Darlings more than others. Libby felt a little strange about being singled out, but she knew that the work they were doing was just too important for them to worry about what other people thought. Others (like Leona) felt humiliated by it and couldn't seem to get past it. Of course, Libby was hopeful that someday maybe the truth would come out. But if it didn't, well, that was okay, too. Mostly because it had to be.

CHAPTER
4

Libby hurried back to the Little Dipper Dorm alone. She had her one free afternoon each week on Lunarday, and she usually waited for Gemma to finish whatever conversation she was having after class so that the two could head back together. But not that day. She pushed open the door and stepped onto the Cosmic Transporter, which deposited her right in front of room 333. She placed her palm on the hand scanner in the middle of the door. Her handprint was accepted and the door slid open.

"Welcome, Libby," the Bot-Bot voice said.

Entering the bedroom, Libby noticed that the flowers smelled twice as strong as they had that morning. She placed her Star-Zap on her dresser and walked right over to them. It was as if they were beckoning her. She sniffed deeply. *Ahhhhhhhh.* They were just so irresistible. She shook her head. Gemma and Scarlet were so wrong. They smelled just like blushbelles, no doubt about it.

Libby walked over to her side of the room and knelt next to her bed, the pink rug soft and fluffy under her knees. She fished around under the bed, pushed aside the unopened case of glimmerchips, then found what she was looking for. She hooked her fingers around the handle and pulled out a bright pink case. She stared at it for a moment, then undid the clasps and lifted the lid.

The door to the room whooshed open, startling Libby. "What's the deal? You left after class without me," Gemma said, pouting. Then she noticed the open case. "Hey, what's that?" she asked, walking over and dropping to her knees next to Libby. "I mean, I know it's an instrument of some sort, but what kind is it? It's bizarre!"

Libby bristled, running her hands over the keyboard.

"I mean, I think I've played almost every instrument there is," Gemma continued. "But I've never seen this one before in my life."

"It's a keytar," Libby said. "A portable keyboard that you play like a guitar." She lifted it out of the case and hung it around her neck by the pink strap. "See?"

"Ohhhhhh," said Gemma. "So does this mean you're trying out for the band?"

"Maybe," said Libby. "I can't make up my mind."

"Well, *I* am," said Gemma. "I just have to figure out which instrument to bring. I play so many, you know." She walked over to her shelf and began studying her choices: guitar, starflooty, star shakers, pluckalong, clarinet.

Better to play one well than many not so well, Libby thought. She blushed, immediately embarrassed by her unkind thought. *My stars.* What was getting into her these days? She carefully lifted the keytar from around her neck and placed it back in the case. Maybe she wouldn't try out. She wasn't feeling quite right. It was entirely possible that she was coming down with something and could use some rest.

"So are you sure you want to try out with that keyfar thing?" Gemma asked Libby. "It just seems kind of weird." She pointed to her shelf of instruments. "Maybe borrow one of mine instead?" She had a funny look on her face, as if she was a bit surprised at the words that had come out of her mouth.

"Key*tar*," Libby corrected her between gritted teeth. "It's called a keytar," she repeated.

"Do what you like," Gemma said with a shrug. She stared at the jumble of instruments, considering them.

Finally, she grabbed the pair of star shakers. "See you," she said.

That was just the motivation Libby needed. She snapped the case closed and, after a brief pause to give Gemma a head start, headed to Star Quad herself.

Libby's mood improved as soon as she stepped outside. It was a pleasant, sunny Time of Letting Go afternoon with a slight breeze, and she was looking forward to sitting in the grass near the splashing fountain and playing music with her fellow Star Darlings. Plus, she could show Gemma just how amazing and versatile a keytar could be. Her roommate had no idea that the instrument could sound like an organ, an accordion *or* an electric guitar!

Libby stopped in her tracks as she approached the band shell. She had been expecting to see a couple of the Star Darlings – Leona, of course; Sage with her guitar; Vega and her bass; Gemma; maybe even Scarlet with her drum kit; and possibly one or two others. But there were literally dozens of Starling Academy students milling about in Star Quad, singing scales and toting guitars, violins and other instruments. They couldn't possibly all be there to try out for Leona's band, could they? How had they even found out about it?

She spotted Orchid, a girl from her Intro to Wishful Thinking class, practising her starflooty.

"Hey, Orchid, what's going on?" Libby asked her.

Orchid blew a few more notes, then lowered her starflooty. "Hey, Libby," she said in a friendly tone. "Everyone's here to try out for the band!" She glanced down at the pink case in Libby's hand. "Aren't you?"

Could there be tryouts for two bands? Libby wondered. "Who's in charge?" she asked.

"Oh, a third-year named Leona," the girl replied. She pointed to the band shell, where Leona stood, her hands on her hips. She was surveying the crowd, looking confused. "You know, the one with the cool golden hair."

"I know her," said Libby. *What on Starland is going on?* she wondered. Leona had apparently decided to invite the whole school to try out. But why? Libby pushed her way through the crowd to the band shell.

"Hey, Leona," she said. "What's happening?"

Leona spun around. Her hair looked even wilder than usual. "What's going on? I wish I knew!" Her eyes swept the crowd. "*Starf!* How did all these people find out about my tryouts? I didn't want the whole school to show up! This is going to take forever!" She stopped a girl walking by with a trumpet. "How did you hear about this?" she asked her.

The girl looked at Leona like she was crazy. "Is this a joke?" she asked. "From the holo-flyer you sent out to the school, of course." The girl lowered her voice and leaned forward conspiratorially. "So is it true that whoever joins the band gets class credit and can drop music class?" she asked. "That's the rumour."

Leona narrowed her eyes. "I bet you anything Scarlet had something to do with this. This sounds exactly like something she would do to annoy me."

There was a laugh behind them. Leona and Libby spun around to find Scarlet standing there, grinning. "I wouldn't mind taking credit for this madhouse," she said. "But it wasn't me. I'm here to try out!" She pointed a drumstick at her drum kit, which was sitting on the stage. "You think I want all this competition?"

Leona groaned. "I'm going to be the most hated girl in Starling Academy when I have to turn most of these girls down," she said, fretting. Libby nodded in sympathy. It would be awful to have to hurt the feelings of so many of her fellow students. Leona had a sudden realization. "And then no one will come to see the band. That would be terrible!"

Libby pulled her Star-Zap out of her pocket and quickly checked her messages. Oddly enough, she had not received Leona's holo-flyer. A quick poll revealed that neither had Vega, Scarlet or any of the other Star Darlings.

Leona grabbed the arm of a girl who stood nearby, a guitar slung around her neck. "Hey, can you show me the holo-flyer?" she asked. The girl nodded, pulled her Star-Zap from her pocket, and projected the message into the air. Leona read it out loud:

CALLING ALL ROCKERS!

Have you always wanted to play in a band?
Desperately seeking vocalists, drummers, guitarists, melodeon players, bass players, keyboard players –
and more!
Meet at the band shell in Star Quad after school today.
Contact Leona for more details.

"That's so bizarre. I totally hate melodeons! I so clearly didn't send that," she said. "But who did?"

The crowd shifted. Someone was trying to push through. "Excuse me, pardon me," said an adult voice. The crowd parted as a teacher made her way to the bandstand. She was of average height with a round, pretty face, long silver hair parted in the middle and a sweeping red dress with huge pockets. She was a fourth-year professor, and until then, Libby had only seen her from afar.

"Leona?" she said. "Professor Leticia Langtree here. You're just the person I've been looking for. Once an invitation for any type of tryout on school property goes out to the entire school, Starling Academy rules require that it must be overseen by a school official. It's in the Student Manual," she added seriously. "So I'm here to make sure everything goes smoothly and fairly." She fished around in her pocket and pulled out a small silver box. "That's why we always use the Ranker in situations like this. You may have seen it used before in public speaking class. It's the only truly fair way to be able to pick a winner without showing favouritism."

Leona stared at the Ranker. Things were not going the way she had planned, and Libby could see how frustrated that was making her. "When I find out who sent out that holo-flyer, I am going to go supernova on them," she said through gritted teeth. "Not. Funny. At. All."

Professor Leticia Langtree ignored her comment. "So if we're all settled, I'm going to make an announcement explaining how we're going to proceed, and then we'll start the tryouts so we can get out of here before breakfast tomorrow," she told Leona.

"Fine," sputtered Leona. She looked both furious and confused. But it was clear that she really had no choice.

The teacher stepped onto the band shell stage. "Hello, I am Professor Leticia Langtree, and I will be overseeing the band tryouts today. I will be recording you with this machine, called a Ranker, for those of you not yet familiar with it. It will ensure that choosing the band is done in a fair way, showing no favouritism to any student. This machine is able to evaluate each performance and assemble the perfect group of musicians, the group that will sound the best together. The Ranker is unbiased and incorruptible. Please remember that I will have nothing at all to do with the choosing. It is entirely up to the Ranker." She held up the machine and moved it back and forth, scanning the crowd. She looked down at the machine and smiled. "The Ranker now has everyone's names and years in its database and is randomly shuffling them. I will call you to the stage in the order the Ranker determines. You will each have two starmins to perform. The Ranker will indicate when your time is up. You must stop performing immediately."

Leona's shoulders sagged. Though she had accepted the unexpected turn of events, that didn't mean she was happy about it. She turned to Libby with a sigh. "This was just supposed to be a Star Darlings band!" she said. "A way for us to have fun and spend time together. I don't want to be the lead singer of a band where I don't know anyone!"

She thought for a moment. "I guess this is the best thing to do now that everything got so messed up." She shook her head. "But who sent out that flyer? And why?"

The teacher stepped down from the stage and settled herself on a bench, the Ranker set up beside her. Leona, Libby and Sage sat on a nearby bench to watch.

"Vivica!" she called. A girl with a pale blue fringe walked onstage.

Sage groaned. "Vivica is the meanest girl in school," she whispered to Libby. Libby recognized the girl from her Astral Accounting class. Libby always thought that the permanently sour expression on Vivica's face made her look as if she had just bitten into a bitterball fruit.

Libby watched with interest. She had no instrument. Then Vivica opened her mouth and started to sing.

Leona immediately sprang to her feet. "Hold it right there," she said, cutting her off.

The girl stopped singing, the look on her face more disagreeable than ever.

"Sorry," said Leona, her voice dripping with fake sympathy. "We already have a lead singer. There won't be any singing tryouts today."

The girl stared venomously at Leona. "Oh, yeah?" she said, placing her hands on her hips. "Then why does it say *vocalists* on the holo-flyer?" she insisted.

Leona laughed and shook her head. "I didn't send out that holo-flyer!" she answered, drawing out the words as if Vivica was a small child. "We don't need a lead singer. End of story."

This served to enrage Vivica further. "Well, I'm not leaving until I get a chance to try out!" she screeched.

"Next!" Leona shouted, her face red. The two girls stared angrily at each other, at an impasse.

Meanwhile, Professor Leticia Langtree was busily searching through the Student Manual. She flipped through pages in the air. Finally, she found what she was looking for and stood up. "Leona, it says right here in the Student Manual," she said, stabbing the air for emphasis, "that if the tryouts are held on school grounds, every student has the right to audition for every position. That means that every position is up for grabs. The Ranker will decide who will be the lead singer of this band. You simply can't choose yourself."

Leona looked stunned. "Wait a starsec. Are you telling me I have to try out for my own band?" she asked incredulously.

The teacher shrugged. "I am," she said. She smiled at Leona. "Good luck!"

Leona's mouth opened and closed, but no sound came out. It looked as though when she regained her power of speech, there was a very good chance she could say something she might regret. Libby grabbed Leona's hand and pulled her down to sit on the bench. "Don't worry," Libby told her. "You'll win this one fair and square." She only hoped she was right.

Vivica smirked at Leona, then began to sing. Libby was grudgingly impressed. The girl's voice was clear and strong. Leona tried to be nonchalant, but Libby noticed that she sat on her hands, quite possibly so she wouldn't start biting her nails from sheer nervousness.

After two starmins, the Ranker let out a loud beep, signalling that her time was up. The tryouts began in earnest: another singer (not as good, and she forgot some words) and a guitar player and a drummer, neither of whom were particularly outstanding.

"Leona!" called the teacher.

Libby glanced at Leona, certain she would be too worked up to perform. But she had underestimated Leona's showmanship. The girl stood, smoothed her golden skirt and made her way to the stage. She really had a great voice, though Libby recognized that her range was limited. She more than made up for that with sheer enthusiasm. The crowd began to clap along, which Leona clearly loved. She had such presence on the stage that it was almost impossible to look away. When she was done, a couple of girls in the audience gave loud whistles of approval. Libby noted with a chuckle that Leona was the only performer who had taken a bow – a deep one – when she was finished.

Leona walked back to the bench, a grin on her face. "And that's how it's done," she said cockily, still keyed up from her brief performance. She looked around. "Well, I guess I'll just go," she said. "Clearly I'm not needed at my own tryouts."

"Arista!" Professor Leticia Langtree called out. A girl staggered onto the stage, carrying a huge tuba. She could barely stand upright.

"Oh," said Leona, clearly intrigued. "Well, maybe just one more...." She plopped down next to Libby on the bench. And there she sat for the rest of the afternoon.

As their names were called, one by one, each girl got up on the band shell stage and played her instrument or sang. Some were full of confidence but not quite so full of talent. Some were shy but good. And a couple were pretty bad, truth be told. Finally, it was Libby's turn. She slung her keytar over her shoulder and walked to the middle of the stage. She had been intending to play a current popular song when she had a sudden flash of inspiration. She laughed out loud at her idea. Flipping the keytar switch to make her instrument sound like an old-timey organ, she began to play a simple but snappy jingle that had played on holo-billboards everywhere when she was a kid.

"If you like to smile

And really hate to frown,

Then get yourself a Sparklebrush.

It's the best toothlight in town!"

she sang, then launched into the chorus.

"Oh, Sparklebrush! Sparklebrush!

How I love you so.

You leave my teeth so clean and white

With that special sparkle glow!"

Libby grinned as everyone instantly laughed with recognition and started singing along. The audience cheered as Libby left the stage.

Leona stood up and punched her in the arm excitedly. "Hey, that was cool," she said. "A blast from the past!"

"Scarlet!" called the teacher. Scarlet made her way to the band shell and pushed her drum kit to the middle of the stage. She sat down, twirled her drumsticks in the air and started playing. Even Leona had to admit – begrudgingly – that the Starling had talent. A lot of it, actually.

Then there were some novelty acts. A first-year held up a triangle and hit it – *Ding! Ding-ding-ding! Ding!* – over and over again until her two starmins was up.

A third-year stepped onto the band shell stage, supporting a huge silver instrument that snaked around her body and had three large horns sprouting from it.

"Is that a ... googlehorn?" Leona whispered to Libby incredulously.

"I do believe it is!" said Libby.

The girl began to play the instrument proudly. Its deep bass blare was actually pretty impressive, but Libby was doubtful that there was any way to incorporate that sound into a cohesive rock band.

Another girl was the proud owner of an ancient timpanpipe, which some of the girls had never even heard of before. The last person Libby had heard expressing admiration for the instrument was her dear departed great-grandmother. Its scratchy-whistly sound made everyone realize why the instrument had fallen out of favour. It was haunting. And not in a good way.

Then a couple of Star Darlings tried out in a row. Sage played the guitar very well. Vega played the bass, and she was quite good, too. Gemma got up and shook her star shakers enthusiastically. Libby caught Leona wincing, though she tried to pass it off as having something in her eye. Libby wasn't fooled.

"Well, that's it!" said Professor Leticia Langtree. She stood, turned off the Ranker and slipped it into her voluminous pocket. "So I'll take this back and determine the results. I'll post them on the holo-announcement board by Halo Hall as soon as I can."

Leona slumped on the bench. "I'm exhausted," she said. She pointed to the Celestial Café, where a large star above the door flashed, indicating that it was dinner-time. "Let's go eat."

She and Leona walked over to the moving pavement. They stepped on and stood in silence for a moment.

"I'm still wondering who sent that holo-flyer out with my name on it," mused Leona. "I'm not fully convinced it wasn't Scarlet."

"It wasn't me," someone behind them said wearily.

Leona jumped. "Why are you always lurking behind me?" she complained. "It's kind of creepy, you know."

Gemma ran up to join them. "That was so much fun! I hope I make it," she said, rattling her star shakers for emphasis. "It would be so awesome to be in a band." She spotted Tessa on the moving pavement ahead. "Tessa, wait up!" she called as she took off after her.

Leona leaned over and whispered in Libby's ear. "I obviously have no idea who's going to make it or not," she said. "Or even if *I* will. But I think it's pretty clear that Gemma is out of the running. There were so many better musicians." She looked at Libby and shrugged.

"Good," Libby heard herself say.

Leona's mouth fell open. "Good?" she repeated. "You're happy about that? I don't get it. I thought you guys were great friends."

Libby bit her lip. "I – I don't get it, either," she said. "I'll see you later." She stepped off the pavement and headed towards her dormitory on foot. She had lost her appetite. Why in the world was she pleased that her roommate had most likely not made the cut? What on Starland was wrong with her?

CHAPTER
5

Once in her peaceful room, Libby tried to distract herself, but she wasn't having an easy time of it. She refolded all of her already neatly folded clothing, then pulled holo-book after holo-book off her shelves, but nothing kept her interest. She just couldn't stop thinking about her ungracious reaction to Leona's news. She was about to call her best friend from home for a pep talk when her Star-Zap beeped. She rolled over and picked it up. The familiar message made her heartbeat quicken.

S.D. WISH BLOSSOM IDENTIFIED. PROCEED TO LADY STELLA'S OFFICE IMMEDIATELY.

Libby jumped out of bed, shoved her feet into a pair of shoes and headed out of the door.

Once outside, she discovered it was lightfall, the magical time of day when the sun begins to disappear and everyone's glow is at its brightest. Starlings got an extra burst of energy at lightfall; whether it was from being surrounded by shimmering Starlings or a direct result of their own personal glow, Libby wasn't quite sure. Perhaps a combination of both. She breezed past groups of classmates chatting on the moving pavement as they returned from dinner.

"Where are you going, Libby?" someone called.

"Hey, where's the fire?" shouted another.

Libby just laughed and waved. She could never explain to them what was going on. Imagine if she told them the truth. "Oh, it's no big deal. I'm just on my way to Lady Stella's office. There's a one-in-eleven chance that I'm going to be on my way to Wishworld before you're even dressed tomorrow morning!"

By dodging oncoming students, she soon caught up with her fellow Star Darlings, who were making their way to Halo Hall, where Lady Stella's office was located. Tessa was still eating a cocomoon. She took a big bite, the milky-white iridescent juice running down her arm.

"Where were you, roomie?" asked Gemma.

To Libby, Gemma's voice sounded accusatory. For a brief second, Libby was fearful that Gemma somehow knew she had been unkind. But as Libby's pulse began to slow down, she realized she was overreacting. "Oh, I wasn't hungry," she said.

"Well, that's just crazy talk," said Tessa with a laugh, holding up the half-eaten cocomoon.

Libby fell into step with the group, grazing shoulders with Adora. Everyone was making small talk, not mentioning where they were heading, or for what purpose, in case anyone was within earshot. But they couldn't keep still – eyes were darting, fingers were tapping, the nervous energy was palpable. They couldn't wait to find out who would be going to Wishworld next.

Sage turned around, and Libby was surprised to see that her eyes were flashing. Even she, who had been through this already and knew for certain that she would not be chosen, seemed to be filled with nervous excitement.

The moving pavement took the girls straight to Halo Hall, and they headed up the stairs and inside, their feet echoing in the empty hallways as they walked past silent classrooms. They filed into Lady Stella's office. The headmistress sat behind her desk, her arms folded. She looked remarkably calm. Libby sat down at the round table, placing her hands on its cool silver surface. It calmed her down – a bit. A few Star Darlings stood, fidgeting nervously. Maybe they were too anxious to sit down, or maybe they wanted a head start when Lady Stella opened the door that led down the stairs to the Wish Cavern.

Once everyone was settled, Lady Stella stood up. "Hello, my Star Darlings," she said. "As you are aware, one of you is about to be chosen for the second Wish Mission. A good Wish Orb is glowing, and it is especially suited to one particular student's strengths. Please don't be upset if you are not chosen today. You will each get your turn."

The Star Darlings all understood that. Still, Libby knew that they all must feel exactly as she did. They wanted it to be theirs. (Except, perhaps, Cassie, who looked slightly miserable. She had confessed to Libby as they sipped sparkle juice in the Lightning Lounge one evening that she wasn't in a rush to head down to Wishworld. She needed some time to get used to the idea. It was pretty clear to Libby that she had not yet.)

"When do we get to go to the caves?" Scarlet asked impatiently.

Lady Stella smiled. "Things are going to happen a little differently this time," she said. "I have been informed by our Wish-Watcher that we will not be going to the Star Darlings Wish Cavern this evening."

The girls began to murmur. Not going to the Wish Cavern! The last time, when Sage was chosen, Lady Stella had opened a hidden door in her office wall, and a secret staircase had been revealed. The girls had headed underground into the secret caves beneath the school. Lady Stella had led them to a secret door. When it opened they had found themselves in a beautiful Wish-House built just for them.

"But, Lady Stella," said Vega, "then how are we going to find out who the Wish Mission is intended for?"

"The Wish Orb will come to you this time," Lady Stella said mysteriously. "Please take a seat so we can begin." She gestured towards the large round silver table that sat in her office.

Once everyone was settled, Lady Stella continued. "Now close your eyes," she said. "When you open them, a Wish Orb will be floating in front of each of you. Everyone, that is, but Sage, since she already went on her mission."

Sage nodded and smiled – a little sadly, Libby thought. Maybe she secretly hoped to be able to go back down again on another mission and do it perfectly this time.

"But only one is the true Wish Orb. The rest are just illusions and will disappear before your eyes."

Libby looked around the table. Everyone's eyes were already closed, so she quickly squeezed hers shut, too. Her stomach was dancing with flutterfocuses. What if she was chosen? Then again, what if she wasn't? The wait seemed interminable. Finally, she heard Lady Stella say, "Open your eyes, Star Darlings!"

There was a collective gasp around the table. Eleven glowing Wish Orbs were floating in the air in front of them. Libby stared at her orb longingly. It looked quite real, pulsing with a gorgeous golden light. But was it just an illusion?

She looked at her fellow Star Darlings. Each girl was staring at her Wish Orb, wondering if it was about to disappear. One by one, Scarlet's, Gemma's, Tessa's, Leona's and Vega's faces crumpled as their orbs disappeared. Cassie let out a gasp – perhaps of relief – as hers vanished. Libby stared at her orb, then stole a quick glance around the table. All the others were gone. She started breathing again.

"It's Libby!" cried Sage. "Good for you!"

Lady Stella walked over and placed her hands on Libby's shoulders. "The Wish Orb has chosen." She peered down at Libby, a gentle smile on her face. "And I think it has chosen wisely. I have a good feeling about this, Libby."

Libby's mouth felt dry. "Thank you," she barely managed to whisper. She pushed her seat back from the table and stood up.

Lady Stella burst into laughter, pointing to Libby's feet. "I'm guessing you were in a big rush to get here?" she asked.

Libby nodded and looked down. She was wearing her fluffy bedroom slippers!

The Star Darlings roared with laughter. Was it because it was so funny to see ladylike Libby wearing silly slippers in public, or were they mostly letting off steam after the last tense few starmins? Libby wasn't sure. But after a moment, she joined in with the laughter, too.

Long after the other girls had left to get ready for bed, Libby returned to the Little Dipper Dormitory, yawning a jaw-cracking yawn as she shuffled along in her slippers. She had stayed behind for final lessons in outfit picking and shooting-star riding and had received some last-starmin Wisher identification tips.

The campus was still and empty, and she watched as lights began to turn off in the dorm, which loomed ahead of her. Libby looked up to see a clear sky full of stars.

She bent her head back and took it all in. It was so amazing that someone as small as her, in the grand scheme of the world, was about to embark on such a huge adventure. Her Star-Zap began to ring. She pulled it out of her star-shaped pocket to see that it was her parents, again.

Her parents popped up in the darkness ahead of her, wearing silk bathrobes. Her mother's hands were placed in matching anti-aging pods, as they were every night before she went to sleep.

"Hi," Libby said.

"Hi, sweetheart," they said in unison. Her mother peered at her. "What are you doing outside?" she asked.

"Shouldn't you be getting ready for bed?" her father added.

"I ... um ... was studying late," Libby said. It was technically the truth.

"Well, it's time to get ready for bed," said her mother. "Listen, we just wanted to see if you had changed your mind about the holiday. There's still time."

Libby sighed. "I'm sorry. I haven't."

Her mother sighed as well.

"All right, we'll figure it out somehow. So, anything exciting happen today, starsweetie?" her father asked.

Libby almost laughed. Anything exciting? Only the most thrilling thing in the history of Starland was all.

She scoured her mind for some bit of information to share. "Well, I, um, tried out for a rock band," she said. "I played the keytar."

"Oh, that's fun," said her father. "Good luck."

"I hope you make it," her mother added. "All those years of classical piano lessons will finally pay off."

"Thanks," Libby said. She was suddenly seized with an odd feeling – a mixture of longing, excitement and a little bit of fear. Part of her wanted to hop into a Starcar, head to Radiant Hills and have her parents tuck her into bed. The other was thrilled to be setting off on an unknown, mysterious, top-secret adventure. "Mummy and Daddy?" she said.

"Yes," her parents perked up. Libby never called them Mummy and Daddy any more.

"I miss you," she said. She had a sudden idea. "I know – I'm going to try to find out a way to combine the holidays. Maybe I can do some volunteering on Glamora-ora. And maybe Aunt Kit could come, too?"

Her parents smiled widely, looking both relieved and happy. "That would be lovely, Libby," her mother said gently.

"Really lovely," her father added.

Libby stopped under a lamppost outside the Little Dipper Dormitory door. "Goodnight," she said softly.

"Goodnight, starsweetie," her parents said together.

It had been really difficult to talk to her parents and not share the exciting, world-changing thing she was about to do. But she still felt better just seeing them and hearing their voices.

The Cosmic Transporter dropped her off at her door, and she gently placed her hand on the scanner. "Good evening, Libby," the voice said in the hushed tones reserved for after-dark hours. She walked into the unlit room. Gemma was already asleep and the starry curtain that divided the room was drawn. Libby got undressed and rooted around in her drawers to find her favourite old pair of pyjamas. They were a little snug, and her ankles and wrists stuck out. But they were warm and cosy and reminded her of home. Vaguely comforted, she nestled between the covers and drifted off to sleep.

CHAPTER
6

Libby stepped off the Flash Vertical Mover and walked towards the hidden door that opened onto the private Star Darlings section of the Wishworld Surveillance Deck. She pushed down her safety starglasses, then walked onto the deck. She was pleased to notice that her fellow Star Darlings were bathed in a pretty rosy glow through her pink lenses.

"Hey, Libby!"

"Over here!"

"Way to go, Libby!"

Libby was immediately mobbed by her fellow Star Darlings, all wearing different-coloured safety starglasses that matched their outfits. Apparently, being chosen for the next mission had turned her into a momentary celebrity. She grinned at everyone, pleased that they had come to see her off.

Astra pushed to the front of the crowd. "How can you stand it?" she practically shouted. "You're about to set off on the biggest adventure of your life and you're as cool as a calaka!"

"Are calakas really cool?" wondered Vega. "I've always wondered where that expression came from."

Libby shrugged. While she might have looked calm on the outside, she certainly didn't feel that way. It felt like a bunch of flutterfocuses were having a dance party in her stomach. She glanced at the far end of the deck and saw the Star Wranglers trying to spot a shooting star heading their way. They would use their lassos to grab it; then they would attach Libby to it and she would be on her way to Wishworld to start her adventure. *Gulp.*

Leona walked up to her, a grin on her face. "Any last words?" she joked. She threw an arm around Libby's neck. "Hopefully by the time you get back, they'll have posted the results from the band tryouts." She let go of Libby and tapped her elbows together three times for luck.

The what? thought Libby. *Oh, that's right, the band tryouts.* That seemed so long ago and so inconsequential to Libby at the moment. "Yes, I hope so," she said. "Good luck."

"Star salutations," said Leona kindly.

One by one, Libby's fellow Star Darlings hugged her, tapped their elbows, and offered unsolicited last-starmin advice. Libby smiled and thanked them all politely, but her mind was elsewhere. She had a moment of panic when she thought she had forgotten her Wish Pendant, but there it was, around her neck, where she had carefully put it that morning. Wait, where was her – oh, there, her Star-Zap was in her pocket. *Relax,* she told herself. *Everything is going to be okay.*

Finally, she made it to the end of the platform, where Lady Stella was waiting.

The headmistress gave Libby a warm smile and embrace, and Libby could feel her tension begin to ebb. Lady Cordial pushed through the crowd to hand Libby a pink backpack with a stuffed glittery pink star attached to the zipper so she would blend in on Wishworld. Libby put her arms through the straps. She made a face. It felt kind of uncomfortable.

Sage pushed forward. "No, silly, you wear it on your back," she said kindly. She removed the backpack and helped Libby put it on correctly. That was better.

"Star salutations, Sage," said Libby gratefully.

"Everything is going to be fine," said Sage, putting a comforting hand on Libby's arm.

"Now, Libby," Lady Stella said, "you are going to do a great job." She pointed to Libby's necklace. "Just remember to keep an eye on your Wish Pendant. It has enough wish energy inside for you to use your secret power. Use it wisely."

"I will," Libby said.

"You also need to watch the Countdown Clock on your Star-Zap. If the wish is not granted before the clock runs out of time, the orb will fade and the mission will fail. And no wish energy will be collected."

Libby nodded. "I understand."

"We'll be monitoring your levels from here. If we think you may be in trouble, we'll send down back-up."

"Okay," said Libby. She was hoping she wouldn't have to rely on anyone's help, but it was nice to know it was there if she did need it.

"The ride down will be fast. Don't forget to change your appearance before you touch down on Wishworld," Lady Stella reminded her.

"I won't," said Libby solemnly.

"Shooting star spotted!" called the Star Wrangler.

Libby felt numb as she watched the wrangler toss out a silver lasso of wish energy and expertly nab a shooting star. Luckily, everyone had on their safety starglasses, because it was so bright it was almost blinding, throwing off a shower of sparks. "You're on!" the wrangler called, struggling to hold the star in place. Her heart nearly thumping out of her chest, Libby stepped forward to the edge of the Surveillance Deck, where she was attached to the star.

"Ready for take-off?" asked the wrangler.

"Ready!" said Libby.

"Libby! Libby!" Libby turned her head and saw Sage fighting her way to the edge of the balcony. "I just remembered something! When my mission started going wrong, I started feeling really –"

Whoosh! The wrangler released the powerful star, and Libby's head was thrown back as it took off. She was on her way as quick as she could say Jack Starling (an old expression of her great-grandmother's, which oddly came to mind at that moment).

What had Sage been about to say? She had felt really hungry? Angry? Sad? Hopefully, Libby wouldn't find out.

Whoa! She hadn't realized what a bumpy ride it would be down to Wishworld! Her long pink hair whipped back as she sped down, down, down. She stared out at the swirling air around her, almost hypnotized by the shifting colours, the intense glow and flashes of light.

Just then she remembered her Star-Zap. She fished it out of her pocket and realized that it was blinking.

Libby snapped back to reality. COMMENCE APPEARANCE CHANGE, the screen read. APPROACHING WISHWORLD ATMOSPHERE. *Oh, starf.* How long had the Star-Zap been trying to remind her? It was flashing really intently, surely an indicator that she had been ignoring it for a while.

Quickly, she accessed the Wishworld Outfit Selector, and she was instantly dressed. She looked down at the outfit Lady Stella had helped her choose the night before. Pink denim skirt, pink-and-white-striped leggings, pink flats and a pink shirt with white polka dots. A white jean jacket completed her Wishling ensemble. She smiled. *Adorable!*

Next step: skin and hair. She placed her hand on her star necklace and recited the words that would start the transformation: "Star light, star bright, the first star I see tonight: I wish I may, I wish I might, have the wish I wish tonight." A wonderful, warm, comforting feeling began to flow through her, and she focused first on her body. She visualized her smooth pale skin devoid of any glitter. Next she pictured plain brown hair instead of her beautiful sparkling pink tresses. (That was a tough one for her, and she was happy to notice that a streak of pink remained.) The star sped up for a moment as it swerved around a meteorite, and she watched in dismay as the sparkles were swept right off her skin. She felt very dull indeed. But now she was ready.

PREPARE FOR LANDING, read her Star-Zap. Libby shot through the clouds and began hurtling towards Wishworld. She closed her eyes as the ground rushed up to meet her. Nobody had told her how scary that would be! But to her relief, she touched down gently. When she opened her eyes, she was pleased to discover that the star had brought her to a secluded spot. She picked up the star and folded it neatly, then stowed it in her backpack. It would come in handy to help her get back home; that was for sure! She scooped up her Star-Zap, which lay on the ground beside her, and stuck it in her pocket. It was only then that she took a closer look at her surroundings. Everything was so lovely, bathed in pink light! Then she laughed as she realized she had forgotten to take off her safety starglasses. Things weren't quite so rosy any more. Instead of the beautiful park that Sage had described landing in, Libby discovered that she was in a dreary alley, and there was a large green metal container that really stank. She could hardly breathe! She held her nose and peeked inside, morbidly curious to discover what on Wishworld could make such a terrible smell. It was filled with rubbish! Papers and wrappers and leftover food scraps and used drink containers, as well as other unidentifiable items in various degrees of decay. She looked away. What a mess! Then she remembered learning in class that Wishlings did not have disappearing rubbish as they did on Starland, and she felt very sorry for them. She caught another whiff and realized that at the moment, she felt sorry for herself. She held her breath and scurried out of the alley.

Libby pulled out her Star-Zap and said, "Take me to the Wisher I've come to help." Directions appeared and Libby quickly fell into step behind an adult female Wishling. After a couple of turns, she found herself on a busy city street. She stood still for a moment and tried to take it all in. It was loud, crowded, overwhelming and totally wonderful all at the same time. Then someone bumped right into her, nearly knocking her over onto the pavement.

"Out of the way, kid," said a gruff voice. "You can't just stop in the middle of the pavement!"

Libby looked up to see an adult male Wishling in a matching jacket and trousers, a thin strip of material tied around his neck. He was holding a brown satchel in one hand and what looked like a very early prototype of a Star-Zap to his ear with the other. He scowled at her. "Oh, just some dumb kid," he said into the phone before he took off, weaving through the crowd.

Libby stuck out her tongue at his departing back. *How rude!*

"Oh, don't mind him," said a voice. Libby looked over to see an adult female Wishling with a kind face pushing a large wheeled contraption with a tiny baby sleeping inside. "Some people have no manners."

Libby smiled at her. "Thank you!" she said. She decided to make her first mental note. By pressing a button on her Star-Zap, she could record in her Cyber Journal observations made in her head. It could then be studied by the other Star Darlings for use on their missions.

Mission 2, Wishworld Observation #1: Some Wishlings are rude. And some are quite nice.

Hmmm ... maybe that wasn't such a mind-blowing observation. It was actually a lot like life on Starland. She knew she should probably get to the school as soon as possible, but she needed a starmin to take it all in. She moved out of the way and watched. Pedestrians rushed by, and people were spilling out of underground stairwells and onto the street. *Where did they come from?* she wondered. *Do some Wishlings live underground?* There were tons of those funny-looking Wishling vehicles – some long and boxlike, filled with lots of people, and some small and carrying only a few.

Many of them were yellow and had signs and lights on the top. The streets were lined with large buildings with glass fronts. There were a lot of shops selling clothes, shoes and food. There were many places called banks and others called pharmacies. And it was noisy: vehicles were honking, revving and screeching. People were yelling, chatting, whistling and constantly moving, moving, moving. She thought she could stand there all day watching the people walk by – wearing their Wishling clothes, their Wishling shoes, talking in their Wishling voices.

Mission 2, Wishworld Observation #2: Wishlings seem to always be in a big rush to get somewhere else.

An official-looking Wishling, wearing a blue uniform with a badge and a matching blue hat on his head, stopped in front of Libby. "Shouldn't you be in school, young lady?" he asked.

Libby snapped out of her reverie. "That's right!" she said. "Thank you!"

She flipped open her Star-Zap (which looked enough like the devices everyone else was using that she wasn't afraid of standing out) and accessed the directions. She began to walk to the school. She quickly figured out the flashing signs on the street corners. The red-lighted hand meant stop and the little white-lighted person walking meant it was okay to cross the street.

The rest of her walk was uneventful (though she did start to wonder why Wishlings needed quite so many banks and those mysterious pharmacy places), and she soon stood across the street from her destination, waiting for the little walking man to tell her it was okay to cross. It was a white-brick building with a flagpole in front, the starred and striped flag fluttering in the breeze. It looked a little shabby, but in a nice way, like it was well used. WELCOM TO OUR SCHOOL read big cut-out letters that hung in the large windows facing the street. That puzzled Libby. *Maybe they spell words differently on Wishworld*, she thought.

"Hurry up," someone called. Libby looked up to see an adult female Wishling in a bright yellow vest and a white hat and gloves beckoning for her to cross the street. "You're late for school!" she said.

Libby did as she was told and hurried to the school entrance. She pushed open the front door and stepped inside. A large letter Ɛ was lying on the floor by the windows. Curious, Libby picked it up. Actual paper! It was very light. She tried to stick it back in the window after the M, but as soon as she turned, it fluttered back to the ground.

"Don't worry about that. I'll fix it later. Don't want anyone to think we don't know how to spell here!"

someone said in a jolly voice. It was an adult female Wishling in a blue uniform that looked just like the one worn by the Wishling who had asked Libby if she should be in school. She held open a door that led to the school lobby. "I'm sorry to say that you're going to need a late pass."

"A late pass, of course," replied Libby. *What on Starland is a late pass?* she wondered.

Libby walked inside, and the Wishling followed her and took a seat behind a desk. She pushed some papers to the side, pulled out a binder, and flipped it open. She picked up a pen and looked up at Libby expectantly.

"Name?" she said. She peered at Libby closely. "Actually, come to think of it, you don't look familiar to me," she said with a frown. Then she smiled despite herself. "Mmmmm, chocolate cake," she said. "My grandpa used to make one every Saturday, with vanilla icing and sprinkles. And then, after dinner, he would light a candle and sing 'Happy Birthday' to me, because I liked birthdays so much. And we'd each eat a big piece with a tall glass of milk."

Libby didn't smell anything, so she just smiled. *Oh, that's right!* Whenever Starlings were around, adult Wishlings smelled the scent of their favourite bakery treat from their childhood. That was a little weird, but mostly kind of nice, she thought. Libby glanced at the name on the woman's badge. Then she leaned forward and looked into the woman's brown eyes, just as Sage had taught her. "Lady Jones," she began. "I am –"

"Lady Jones!" the adult female Wishling said with a cackle. "Do you think I'm royalty? That's Officer Jones to you, young lady!"

Oops. Libby started over. "Officer Jones, I am Libby, the new student," she said. She felt a rush of relief when the Wishling repeated, "You are Libby, the new student."

She smiled as Officer Jones wrote *Libby* on the late pass. Then Officer Jones looked up. "Last name?"

Libby opened her mouth, then closed it. They hadn't covered this in school. Starlings didn't have last names. "It's Libby ... uh ... Libby...."

In a panic, she glanced down at a folded piece of paper on the officer's desk and saw a list. A class list, maybe? She read aloud the first word she saw, which was not easy, as it was upside down. "Li ... li ... liverwurst," she said. That was when she realized that the piece of paper was not a class list. It was a menu.

She regretted her choice as soon as she said it out loud. She wasn't quite sure what it was, but she did know one thing for certain: it was a terrible-sounding name!

"Libby ... Liverwurst?" the officer said, frowning.

"Libby Liverwurst," Libby repeated glumly.

With a shake of her head, the officer wrote down the name on the late pass. "Libby Liverwurst." She looked like she was trying hard not to smile. "And what class are you in?"

"Room 546," she said, recalling the number she had read on the directions.

"Room 546," repeated the officer, writing down the numbers. She handed Libby the pass. "Have a good day, Miss Liverwurst."

"Thank you," said Libby politely.

Once she was out of the officer's view, Libby pulled out her Star-Zap and followed the directions it provided. *Up two flights, through the doors, make a left, past the gym, first classroom on the right.* The hallway was quiet, but she could hear the drone of teachers' voices from behind closed classroom doors and the higher-pitched voices of the kids. Then she caught the squeaking sound of rubber soles on wood. That had to be from the gym. She noted that the walls were painted a cheerful shade of yellow. By each doorway was a large rectangular board, covered in artwork – busy scenes, funny faces, drawings of odd creatures she had never seen before. There were also several colourful posters hanging on the walls. One had a simple white background with the words

AVA FOR PRESIDENT on it in large letters. Nothing else. Another really caught her eye. On it was an image of a bearded adult male Wishling, in a red, white and blue outfit and top hat, pointing directly at her. I WANT YOU TO VOTE FOR KRISTIE! it read.

Interesting. Libby had a secret desire to get involved in school politics and hoped one day to run for Light Leader, the head of the student government of Starling Academy. She glanced at the bottom of the poster and noticed that the election was to be held in two days' time. *Hmmm.* Maybe she'd learn a few tricks about elections while she was here. As well as granting a wish and collecting a vast amount of wish energy, of course.

She glanced up and realized she had passed the classroom she was looking for, room 546. She backtracked, and then, taking a deep breath, she knocked and waited.

The door opened, and a teacher with a sweet round face and short curly brown hair looked down at her curiously. Libby remembered her line. Before the teacher could say a word, she announced, "I am Libby, your new student."

To Libby's relief, the teacher ushered her right in (after sniffing the air and exclaiming how it smelled just like red velvet cake, that is). "Class, this is Libby, our new student," she told everyone. She pointed to an empty desk at the back of the room. "You can sit right there," she said.

Libby made her way down the aisle, looking at the students curiously. The kids all had different skin colours, just like at home. And when she pictured them with brightly coloured hair – reds, oranges, yellows, greens, blues and purples – and a layer of glitter on their skin, they looked an awful lot like Starlings. Wishlings and Starlings weren't that different at all.

She settled herself into her seat, noting how uncomfortable Wishling school furniture was.

"My name is Ms Blackstone," the teacher said. "And you are Libby...."

Great. This again. "Liverwurst," Libby said miserably.

As she had feared, the class burst into laughter.

"Class!" said the teacher. "I am very disappointed in you. We don't laugh at people's names! That is completely unacceptable. Please apologize to Libby Liv – to Libby."

"We're sorry, Libby Liverwurst," the class said in unison.

Libby wasn't certain, but she had a sneaking suspicion that her teacher was trying very hard not to laugh.

"That's okay," said Libby. "It *is* a pretty funny name."

Ms Blackstone had a sympathetic look on her face. "I'm sorry, Libby, but we're about to head out for a class trip. And since you don't have a signed permission slip, you won't be able to come along with us. I'll see if I can get you a seat in Mr Dilling –"

Libby thought fast. She couldn't be separated from her Wisher! "I already gave you the permission slip," she said, looking into the teacher's eyes. "So I *can* come."

Ms Blackstone thought for a moment. "Oh, that's right," she said, nodding. "You already gave me the permission slip. So you can come."

The young male Wishling in the seat ahead of Libby's turned around. "Wait a minute, how did you do that?" he asked.

"Do what?" asked Libby innocently.

At the front of the bus, a small girl, her hair cut close to her head in a very cute shaggy style, stood and knelt on her seat so she faced the rest of the bus. She began to sing:

"*Ninety-nine bottles of beer on the wall....*"

The class cheered and joined in.

"Ninety-nine bottles of beer,
If one of those bottles should happen to fall,
How many bottles of beer on the wall?
Ninety-eight bottles of –"

"Inappropriate!" Ms Blackstone called out from her seat in the front of the school bus.

There was a short silence, then the girl grinned and started singing again.

"Ninety-nine bottles of root beer on the wall, ninety-nine bottles of root beer...."

The class laughed and sang along.

"That's better!" called Ms Blackstone.

Libby took a furtive look at her Wish Pendant. She had taken a seat next to a young female Wishling with curly red hair and freckles who was staring out of the window, a pensive look on her face. Libby was hoping that the young female Wishling's preoccupied look was due to deep thoughts about an unfulfilled wish. But when Libby sat down and introduced herself, she realized that her Wish Pendant was still dark. Not wanting to be rude, she tried to strike up a conversation.

"So what's your name?" Libby asked brightly.

"Susie," she said.

"And where are we going on our class trip?" Libby asked.

"Aquarium," Susie answered.

Libby had no idea what that was, but obviously she couldn't ask. Maybe her next question would clear things up a little. "Um ... what's your favourite thing at the aquarium?"

"Fish," Susie said.

No such luck. Libby nodded, smiling to herself as she realized that she had traded the world's most talkative roommate for the world's least talkative seatmate.

The bus came to a stop at a red light. *Red for stop,* thought Libby. She was getting familiar with the way things worked on Wishworld. A young female Wishling appeared at Libby's side. "Switch seats?" she asked.

"Sure!" said Libby gratefully. She crossed the aisle and sat in the empty seat next to a young female Wishling with long blonde hair and bright blue nail polish. The Wishling grinned at Libby.

"Hi, Libby Liverspots," she said. "I'm Gabby."

Libby didn't correct her, although if there was one name that was less pleasant-sounding than Libby Liverwurst, that had to be it. "Hey, Gabby," she said. She looked down expectantly. Her Wish Pendant was still dark. *Sigh.*

Libby shifted in her seat. It was pretty uncomfortable. She realized that vehicle seats, like those in the classroom, didn't automatically adjust on Wishworld. But surely there was a button or something to push to get a little more comfortable. This was ridiculous. She started to examine her side of the seat.

The young male Wishling across the aisle from her was giving her an odd look.

"What are you looking for, new girl?" he asked. "You lose something?"

"I'm just looking for the seat adjuster," Libby said.

He looked blank.

"To fix the seat for my height and weight," Libby explained. "You know, so I'll be more comfortable."

He laughed. "Comfortable? On a school bus? What kind of buses have you been riding?" He elbowed his seatmate and pointed to Libby. "Hey, Aidan, the new girl is used to adjustable school-bus seats!"

Aidan nodded. "I've heard about those," he said knowingly. "Private school, right?"

"Um, sure," said Libby, confused. She turned back to her seatmate. At least she seemed a little more talkative than the last one. Libby figured she could get some helpful information out of her. "So tell me about our class," she said. "Anything interesting I should know about?"

Gabby thought for a moment. "Well, we're all working on our test papers. So you're going to have to come up with a subject to write about."

Libby thought about that for a moment. Didn't seem promising. "Anything else?"

"We're learning how to square-dance," she said.

Aidan groaned. "She wants to know what's interesting, not what's the most hideous thing about school," he said. "Square-dancing is the worst. We all have to hold hands and do-si-do. It is so painful."

Libby nodded sympathetically. She was getting good at pretending she wasn't completely confused by what everyone was saying to her. "So what's going on at school that *is* interesting?" she asked him.

He thought for a moment. "I guess I'd have to say it's the election," he said finally. "Two best friends are running against each other. It's pretty weird."

A wave of electricity ran up Libby's spine. She sat up straight in her seat. Could that be the energy surge that Lady Stella had mentioned? She wasn't sure, but it was a possibility. Maybe she was on to something here!

"That seems tough," Libby said, her voice higher than usual in her excitement. She thought back to the posters in the hallway. "So is either Ava or ... um, Kristie in our class?"

"Ava is," said Gabby.

"So which one is A –" Libby started. But then the bus shuddered to a stop with a loud squealing sound. The kids all immediately jumped to their feet and began pushing in a mad rush to get off the bus.

Libby struggled to keep her balance as she was swept down the aisle. "No pushing each other! No shoving!" said Ms Blackstone, to no avail. "Do you want me to turn this bus around and go back right now?"

Once everyone was off the bus and had listened to a lecture about bus-exiting safety, Ms Blackstone led them down a path to a low concrete building surrounded by a high wall. The air felt different there to Libby – salty, heavy and damp. It smelled different, too – she couldn't quite put her finger on it – kind of pleasant and unpleasant at the same time. She couldn't decide.

Ms Blackstone took a deep breath and smiled. "Ah, I love the smell of the sea," she said. "So briny and refreshing." She turned to the class. "Okay, class," she said. "I need you to stay right here while I sort out our tickets." She headed to the ticket booth while the students milled about on the walkway in front of the building.

Now's my chance to find Ava, thought Libby. Students were standing in groups, chatting. Some young male Wishlings were horsing around, pushing each other and laughing loudly. Libby scanned the crowd. Then she smiled as she spotted a short young female Wishling with a pin-straight brown bob that curved around her chin. Libby was smiling because the young female Wishling was wearing an AVA FOR PRESIDENT T-shirt.

"Hey," said Libby, stepping up to her. "I'm Libby. You must be Ava." She looked down at her Star Pendant, anticipating its golden glow.

But there was nothing.

CHAPTER
7

The young female Wishling laughed. "I'm not
Ava. I'm her campaign manager, Waverly." She reached
into her pocket. "Nice to meet you, Libby. How would
you like a badge?" Without waiting for an answer, she
pressed a round flat object into Libby's hand. Libby
looked down. It said VOTE FOR AVA on it.

"Hi, Waverly," Libby said. "And thanks for the
badge." She had no idea what to do with it, so she
shoved it into her skirt pocket, to Waverly's obvious
disappointment. "So what's a campaign manager?"

Waverly smiled. "I help her write speeches,
make posters, make sure she's following the school's
election rules and convince people to vote for her.
I keep things running and make sure she's focused."

She leaned forward conspiratorially. "And trust me, sometimes she needs it! Basically anything that needs to be done to help get her elected. It's a really important job."

"Interesting," said Libby. She wondered who she would ask to be her campaign manager – if she ever ran for office, that is. Maybe Leona. She would be able to get lots of attention; she loved being in the spotlight.... Scratch that. Leona would probably want to run for Light Leader herself!

"So where's the candidate?" Libby asked Waverly.

"She's in the bathroom," said Waverly. "She should be out in a minute." She leaned forward again. "So can we count on your vote?"

Libby laughed. "Shouldn't I meet Ava first?"

Waverly peered at Libby, a scowl on her face. "Trust me, when you meet her, you'll see she is the perfect person for the job."

Mrs Blackstone walked back to the group. "We're good to go," she told them, brandishing a stack of tickets. "Now everyone walk single file through the turnstile. We'll have a couple of minutes to explore a bit before we head to the sea lion show."

Libby immediately perked up. Sea glions? She didn't know glions could swim! She thought the big cats hated the water. This would be very interesting indeed.

The students were eager to get inside and began pushing again. "One at a time!" Ms Blackstone warned. "Everyone take your turn!" She waggled a finger at them. "If there is any more pushing, I promise that this will be the very last field trip we take!"

Libby approached the turnstile with trepidation. It looked like that metal bar was going to hurt when she banged into it. But it moved down and out of her way easily and the next bar popped up behind her. She stood to the side to watch the other students go through. What a fun machine! She had never seen anything like it before.

When the allure of the turnstile had worn off, Libby realized she was in a room with glass walls. Behind those walls was a lot of water, and in the water were multicoloured creatures in all shapes and sizes, swimming, floating, diving, bobbing. Libby pressed her forehead to the cool glass and stared, completely absorbed and forgetting about best friends and school elections. She had known that there would be some strange creatures on Wishworld, but this was incredible!

"But how do they breathe underwater?" she said aloud.

Aidan, who happened to be standing next to her, laughed. "You're kidding, right? Fish have gills, dummy."

"Of course I'm kidding!" said Libby, slapping Aidan on the back, a little too hard. So those were fish! She realized she should stop asking questions that could compromise her identity. She stared in silence at a vibrant yellow creature as it floated in the water in front of her, its mouth opening and closing, its strange little arm appendages fluttering up and down. It was weird and beautiful. Libby was so enthralled she completely forgot to make any wish observations. She probably wouldn't even have known where to start. There were no fish on Starland. Its waters did not contain life-forms of any kind. It was also odd for her to see creatures in captivity. While she understood that it was probably educational for Wishlings to see them up close, it still made her feel sad to see wild creatures on display. On Starland all living creatures roamed free. Wishworld was getting odder by the starmin.

"Come, class, the sea lion show is about to begin," said Ms Blackstone. "Follow me."

The class obediently followed their teacher out of the door. Libby noted there was no pushing or shoving; apparently the threat of no more field trips had worked. They went down a pathway to an entrance that led into a small open-air stadium with rows of seats surrounding a big pool of water with a platform in the middle.

Libby found herself in the first row, sitting next to Waverly. Even though it was the Time of Letting Go, once she was seated, she discovered that it was warm in the sunlight. Libby removed her jacket.

"Cute outfit," said Waverly appreciatively.

Libby smiled. She and Lady Stella had done a good job.

"Hey, could you scootch over?" Waverly asked. "I want to save Ava a seat."

"Good idea," said Libby. She wasn't quite sure what "scootching" was, but she moved over so there was room between them. Waverly looked satisfied, so Libby assumed she had done the correct thing.

While Libby waited, she stared at the platform, waiting for the glions to appear. Glions were sweet and gentle large creatures with multicoloured shimmering manes of hair around their faces and long, tufted tails. Then she thought she saw, out of the corner of her eye, something moving quickly through the water right in front of her, and started. She peered into the water but didn't see anything. Must have been her imagination.

Waverly searched the crowd. The young female Wishling who had been singing on the school bus stood in the aisle, looking for a seat. "Ava! Ava! Over here!" Waverly shouted, waving wildly to her.

Was Libby seeing things, or did Ava seem to hesitate for a moment before she joined them? The young female Wishling shuffled past other students to squeeze in between Libby and Waverly.

"Ava, this is Libby," said Waverly, "the new girl in class today."

"Oh, yeah," said Ava. "Libby Luncheon Meat!" She elbowed Libby in the side. "Sorry, I couldn't resist."

"That's me," Libby said. She sneaked a look at her Wish Pendant. *Startastic!* It was glowing.

Ava held up a fist and smiled at Libby expectantly. Libby stared at it. She vaguely remembered a Wishers 101 lesson during which they talked about the strange custom many Wishlings followed of shaking hands. So Libby grabbed Ava's fist and shook it. It felt awkward, and Ava confirmed that by laughing.

"Very formal!" she said. "Pleased to meet you, madam!"

Libby realized she had made a mistake. She made a quick note.

Mission 2, Wishworld Observation #3: Figure out mysterious Wishling greeting involving raised fists.

"So do we have your vote?" Waverly asked excitedly.

"Give her a break, Waverly," Ava said, crossing her arms tightly. "We're on a class trip, for goodness' sake."

The two girls gave each other pointed looks.

"Is something wrong?" asked Libby. Her pulse quickened. Maybe that was a clue.

"Nothing's wrong!" said Waverly quickly. "Why would you say that? The campaign is going great!" She narrowed her eyes. "Are you from the school newspaper?"

Ava laughed. She put her hands to the sides of her mouth. "Extra! Extra! Read all about it," she called. "Breaking election news!"

"Excuse me," said a classmate, and they stood to let her pass by. Libby took the opportunity to turn to Ava. "So nothing's wrong?" she asked softly.

Ava glanced quickly at Waverly, who was looking the other way. "Nothing's wrong, really," she said to Libby. "Well ... actually ... I mean...." Her voice trailed off.

"Tell me," said Libby, leaning forward eagerly.

"Well, actually, if you want to know, I was just thinking that I wish I could win...."

"Hello, ladies and gentlemen, boys and girls, and welcome to Applewood Aquarium!" a voice boomed.

Ava snapped to attention, her unfinished wish dangling in the air in front of Libby.

But Libby grinned. *You just wish you could win the class election*, she thought, finishing Ava's sentence. The election was two days away. She sneaked a look at her

Countdown Clock. Forty-eight hours to go. That was two days exactly! That sealed the deal. Libby sat back in her seat with a smile on her face. The pendant had been glowing. She had figured out the wish. Now she just had to figure out how she was going to help make it come true.

But that would have to wait. Right now Libby was going to enjoy the sea glion show.

"Please put your hands together for Trainer Amy, and Felix and Oscar, our trained sea lions!" Libby and the rest of the students cheered and applauded.

An adult female Wishling in a monogrammed turquoise shirt, with a bucket in her hand and a whistle around her neck, ran out onto the platform. She blew the whistle and the strangest thing happened. Before Libby's astounded eyes, two sleek, dark creatures jumped out of the water and sailed through the air past each other before diving back in, hardly making a splash.

"My stars!" Libby cried. "What was that? Some kind of fish?"

Waverly gave her a look. "This is a sea lion show. What do you think they are?"

"Oh," said Libby, still confused. She sat back and took it all in. It turned out that Felix and Oscar were California sea *lions*, a type of marine mammal related to other creatures called seals and walruses. (That seemed to make sense to everyone else, so Libby nodded along with the crowd.) They were smart, they were great swimmers and they loved to eat fish. In fact, Trainer Amy had a bucketful for them. The sea lions could each eat 16 kilos of fish a day. This was a little tough for Libby to hear, as she had been introduced to fish just moments before and was quite charmed by them. Plus, all living creatures on Starland – Starlings and animals alike – were vegetarians, so she had never seen a carnivore before in her life. She looked away as the adorable sea lions wolfed down fish after fish. The audience learned that the seals were actually furry, even though they looked rubbery. They had excellent senses of hearing and smell and special reflecting eyes that helped them see better in the dark ocean. They had a layer of blubber under their skin to keep them warm in the cold water. They could dive up to 182 metres and spend 10 to 20 minutes underwater without needing to take a breath.

And the things they could do! The tricks amazed Libby. She watched as they jumped out of the water with ease and did somersaults in the air. Libby clapped with delight as Oscar balanced a large striped ball on his nose, then tossed it over to Felix, who caught it effortlessly and jumped into the water and started swimming, never dropping it. They could stand on their front flippers and bend their tails to touch their noses. They leapt through a series of hoops, then jumped out of the water, slid neatly across the platform, and climbed up to their perches. Libby cheered along with the crowd. Oscar clapped along to the music as Felix swam quickly around the pool; then Oscar dived in to join him in matching double backflips to end the show.

Splash! Everyone in the first two rows got sprayed in the face. Libby groaned along with the others and grimaced. But truthfully, she was kind of delighted.

Once they had slowly made their way out of the stadium, Ms Blackstone led them to the next stop on their tour – the penguin house. As soon as Libby pushed open the door, she was momentarily stunned by the smell. The warm, moist, stinky air made her eyes water. "Leaping starberries," she muttered to herself. "That's nasty!" As she made her way to the front of the dark room, she found herself face-to-face with another glass wall. When she saw what was behind the glass, she forgot about the stench. For in front of her were the funniest creatures she had ever seen in her life – black and white with pointy beaks, beady eyes, and stubby wings that they held out from their sides as they moved around on the rocks above a pool of water. She watched with delight as they waddled and hopped, ungainly as could be. Waddle waddle waddle waddle. HOP. Waddle waddle waddle waddle. HOP. It made Libby laugh out loud. And then, with one movement, they suddenly transformed themselves from awkward to awesome. They dived into the water and began to zoom around with seemingly reckless speed, yet they never bumped into each other. She found herself switching her attention back and forth between the adorably ungainly penguins on the top half of the exhibit and the graceful swimmers on the bottom. She felt as if she could have stood in the dark exhibit watching those creatures all day. "Aren't they amazing?" she said to the student who had been standing next to her. No answer. He was gone. Blinking slowly, she looked around. The room was empty. The class had left the building without her.

Where did they go? Libby tried to stay calm. She ran into another building and looked around. But they weren't in the jellyfish room (another place Libby could have stayed all day, watching the creatures' slowly waving tentacles and the hypnotic movement of their glowing undulating bodies). She was momentarily distracted by a tank full of almost impossibly cute creatures (the sign said they were sea horses, but Libby thought they should be called galliope-fish), but then she began to search again in earnest. There was no time to linger. She was lost.

Finally, to Libby's immense relief, an adult female Wishling, wearing a turquoise shirt and a whistle around her neck, approached her. It was Trainer Amy. "You look lost," she told Libby. "You're part of that school tour, aren't you?"

Libby nodded.

"Your class is at the touch tank," Trainer Amy said. "I'll take you there." With a sigh of relief, Libby followed obediently behind her. But Trainer Amy stopped for a moment. "Do you smell vanilla cupcakes?" she asked, sniffing the air. Libby smiled and shrugged.

Libby was happy to find her class (and a little put off that no one seemed to have missed her), but she forgot everything as soon as she saw the touch tank. As its name said, it was a large low aquarium filled with sea creatures you could actually touch. Libby rolled up her sleeves and wiggled her way between two students until she had some space at the edge of the tank. She plunged her hands into the water. Luckily, there was a guide who explained what everything was, because it was new to Libby. There were prehistoric-looking horseshoe crabs, shy hermit crabs, slippery sea slugs, bumpy starfish in all sizes, sand dollars, mussels, spiny sea urchins, small sharks and flat stingrays with mouths like suction hoses that glided through the water, flapping their soft wings. Once again she wished she could stay all day.

After Ms Blackstone had made sure that everyone cleaned their hands (by rubbing in some stinky gel, not passing their hands under a warm light as they did at home), they had a quick lunch in the cafeteria and then boarded the bus back to school. On the plus side, Libby had ordered something called a grilled cheese on rye and rather enjoyed it. On the minus side, she had just missed grabbing a seat next to Ava at lunch. She was hoping to sit next to her on the ride home, but to her dismay Waverly beat her to it. Waverly was deep in conversation with Ava, who was listening with a slightly distracted look on her face. Libby chose a seat near the front of the bus and sat down. A cute young male Wishling sat next to her, his sandy brown hair falling into his eyes, and she smiled at him. As soon as the doors folded shut, the skies opened up and it began to pour. Libby was shocked to see rivulets of water run down the windows; apparently, Wishling vehicles did not have the same dry-surround protection that they had on Starland. She was intrigued by the window wipers and watched them intently. Soon the *slish-slosh* of the rain and the steady *whoosh*,

whoosh as the wipers went back and forth combined to make her feel very, very sleepy.

What a great first day! she thought. *I found my Wisher and figured out the wish right away. I'm pretty sure I can help make it come true. And the aquarium was amazing.*

Her last thought before she drifted off to sleep was *Mission 2, Wishworld Observation #4: Don't leave Wishworld without seeing some penguins.*

CHAPTER
8

Libby awoke with a start as the bus pulled to a stop. It took her a moment to remember where she was and what was going on (school bus, Wishworld, wish fulfilment).

"Nice nap?" asked the young male Wishling.

Libby nodded. She felt very refreshed, actually.

After she and her classmates got off the bus and headed to their classroom, they had to scramble to get their bags packed up before the final bell. It was time to go home. Libby, of course, had no place to go home to, so she was up for anything – hopefully something election related.

"Here you go," said Ms Blackstone, walking over to Libby's desk and handing her a thick, heavy book.

"Everyone, your maths homework for tonight is section three, pages 15 through to 17."

Libby's eyes lit up as she grasped the book in her hands. She flipped through the pages, marvelling at the thinness of the paper and the way it was printed on both sides. She hugged the book to her chest.

The girl in the seat in front of her turned around. "Wow," she said. "I've never seen anyone so excited about maths homework before!"

Ava leaned on Libby's desk and zipped up her silvery backpack. "Homework will be the death of me," she groaned. "I wish we didn't have any tonight."

Libby pricked up her ears when she heard the word *wish*. She really wanted her Wisher to be happy. Surely that meant helping her with any extra little wishes that came up when Libby was around. It couldn't hurt to have a happy Wisher; she was sure of it.

This was going to be easy. Libby sidled up to Ms Blackstone and peered into her eyes. "Maybe we shouldn't have any homework tonight," she said quietly.

"I'm sorry, Libby, did you say something?" Ms Blackstone asked distractedly.

Libby glanced around to make sure the other students couldn't hear. "Maybe we shouldn't have any homework tonight," she repeated, more intently this time.

Ms Blackstone nodded. "Maybe we shouldn't have any homework tonight," she said loudly.

The class cheered and happily returned their textbooks to their desks.

"Wow," Libby heard Ava say. "Sometimes wishes do come true. Just like that!"

"Yeah," Libby said to herself with a laugh. "Just like that!"

The bell signalling the end of the day rang, and the students streamed out of the classroom, still cheering. Libby followed along as they merged with other kids in the hallway and marched down the stairs, past the auditorium and out of the door into the yard. She lost sight of Ava and wandered around the schoolyard in search of her, dodging flying balls and running kids. She finally found her and Waverly chatting in the corner of the yard. She couldn't help noticing that Waverly had a look on her face that Libby was beginning to recognize: one of irritation.

"I'm just not sure you're taking this election seriously enough," Libby heard Waverly say. "We missed a whole day of campaigning!" She shook her head. "Did you notice that while we were away, Kristie hung up some new posters? She's got a lot more posters up than us now."

"She did?" said Ava, looking interested. "I must have missed them."

Libby nodded. She had spotted one by the auditorium on her way out. It featured a huge blown-up photo of a young female Wishling with long, straight black hair on a bright green background. She was blowing a big pink bubble – only the bubble was actually a pink balloon that was glued to the poster board. The copy read DON'T BLOW IT, VOTE FOR KRISTIE. Libby joined in the conversation and described the poster to Ava.

Ava laughed out loud. "What a funny idea!" she said. "Kristie always has such –"

"Correction," said Waverly exasperatedly. "It's a lame idea. She's making a joke out of the election. I didn't like them at all. Plus, now she's handing out bubble gum to everyone." She pointed to a boy who was walking by, chomping away, his cheeks stuffed with bubble gum.

"Everyone knows you're not allowed to chew gum on school grounds." She pursed her lips. "She's not following school rules. Maybe I should report her to the –"

"Don't do that," said Ava quickly. "Hey, I have an idea. Let's make some cool posters of our own. I've got all those art supplies at home still."

Yes! That was exactly what Libby was hoping for.

She was excited to see Ava working to make her own wish come true. "I'll help!" she offered.

But the two girls were staring at her expectantly.

"What?" said Libby, shrugging.

"Don't you have to ask your mum first?" Ava asked.

Libby nodded. "Of course!" she said. She opened her Star-Zap and randomly punched in some numbers. To her surprise, it began to ring. She made a hasty observation: *Mission 2, Wishworld Observation #5: Star-Zaps work as actual phones on Wishworld.*

"Hello," said a voice.

Ava and Waverly were watching, so Libby decided to wing it. "Hi, Mum," she said. "Can I go to my new friend's house after school?"

"Sorry, I think you have the wrong number," said the voice on the other end.

Libby had an idea. "Oh, you have a work dinner tonight?" she said. She paused. "Okay, I'll ask."

"Listen, kid, you have the wrong number," the person repeated.

She held her hand over the Star-Zap. "My mum's got a big work dinner tonight that's going to run late, and she was wondering if I could sleep over at your house tonight."

Ava shrugged. "Sure. My mum won't mind."

"Okay, so it's a plan," said Libby. "Thanks, Mum."

"You do realize that you have the wrong number and that I'm not your mother," said the voice. "Actually, I'm not anyone's mother. Because I'm a father!"

Libby almost burst out laughing. "I love you, too, Mum," she answered.

And so it was settled. Libby mentally patted herself on the back the whole walk to Ava's. Everything was going startastically on her mission so far. She'd be collecting wish energy in no time.

"Mum! I'm home!" Ava yelled. No answer. "She must be in her office," she said. "She can never hear me when she's in there." She slipped off her shoes and lined them up by the door. Libby and Waverly did the same. Libby wiggled her bare toes, with their bright pink polish. Obviously Wishling shoes were not made of materials that repelled dirt. And she remembered learning that their homes were not self-cleaning. Poor Wishlings.

Afternoon sunlight streamed through the windows. The three girls spread out their materials on the dining-room table. Ava headed to a big silver box in the kitchen and pulled open the door. The lit interior revealed shelves filled with different foods and drinks.

"Can I get you anything?" she asked. Both Libby and Waverly asked for water.

Mission 2, Wishworld Observation #6: Wishling food apparently does not keep constant optimal temperature and needs to be stored in large cooling devices.

As soon as they were settled, Waverly produced a notebook and a pen from her backpack. "Let's come up with some new slogans," she said.

"I have an idea," Ava said softly. She looked excited to share it. "Hey, remember last Halloween when Kristie and I went as prisoners in those striped costumes? We could take that picture of me and draw bars in front of my face, and the message could be 'Wanted: Ava for President'." She smiled at Waverly expectantly.

"No way," said Waverly. "Too gimmicky. How is anyone going to take you seriously as a candidate?"

Ava's face fell.

Libby thought fast. "Well, then, how about a picture of Ava with a caption?" she suggested. "Something fun and memorable. Like 'Vote for Ava, she's....'" Her voice trailed off. "What rhymes with Ava?"

"How about *favour*?" suggested Ava. "'Do me a favour and vote for Ava'?" She pronounced it "favah".

"That's cute!" said Libby.

Waverly made a face. "That's terrible," she said.

Ava bit her lip and tried again. "'Vote for Ava, she's got flava'?"

"Oh, that's good," said Libby. "Very catchy."

Waverly wadded up a napkin and threw it at Libby's head. "No offence, guys, but those really stink."

Ava didn't look so sure. "I think kids like fun stuff," she said. "It makes them laugh. It's memorable." She looked away. "I know I do. And so does Kristie," she muttered.

"This is no time for jokes. We need to let the students know that you are serious about the job!"

Ava looked down at the table. "Okay," she said.

Waverly stood up. "Can I go to your room to get the supplies?" she asked.

"Sure," said Ava.

Libby put her hand on Ava's arm as soon as Waverly left the room. "I thought those ideas were great," she said. "We should just tell Waverly you want to do something fun. It's your campaign."

Ava shook her head. "No, I guess she's right," she said. "Elections should be serious." She sighed. "Nothing really rhymes with Ava anyway."

"I've got it," Waverly said, returning with a stack of poster board. "No gimmicks, no rhymes and certainly no costumes. We'll take a picture of you, looking responsible. We'll print it in black and white with the words 'Vote for Ava'. Simple. Classic. Effective. Trust me, it's the best way to go."

Ava thought for a moment. "Okay," she finally said.

"Are you sure?" Libby asked worriedly.

"You guys have to trust me," Waverly repeated. "I know what I'm doing."

Libby sighed. She hoped that Waverly was right.

After taking 53 photos of Ava with her phone (Libby counted), Waverly was finally convinced they had the right one. It was "the perfect combination of serious and approachable" per Waverly, although they all looked pretty much the same to Libby, save the one she liked best, in which Ava was crossing her eyes and making a goofy face. Libby had overheard Ava muttering, "I wish this was over," under her breath, so she had concentrated on making sure that the last photo was indeed perfect. They printed 20 black-and-white copies ("Classic and classy," Waverly had proclaimed) and glued them onto the poster boards with the word VOTE on top of the photo and FOR AVA underneath.

Libby turned to Ava. "What do you think?" she asked.

Ava opened up her mouth as if to say something and then shrugged. "They're fine," she said.

Waverly looked down at the posters. "You know," she said, "I think I love them."

"Love what?" someone said.

"Oh, hey, Mum," said Ava. "Waverly was just saying that she loves the campaign posters we made."

Libby looked up. Ava's mum wore black-rimmed glasses and had short red hair, which she pushed behind her ears. She was wearing jeans and a faded red hoodie. She looked at the posters and smiled. "Very nice, girls. A little serious but I guess that's the point. Are you hungry?" She inhaled deeply. "Hey, can anyone else smell spice cake?" She sniffed again. "With ... cream cheese frosting?"

Ava gave her mother a funny look. "This is Libby, the new girl at school. She's helping out with the campaign. She's going to sleep over tonight."

Ava's mum smiled. "Sounds good."

Then she stole a glance at the large timepiece that hung on the wall. "Yikes!" she said. "Sorry, I was busy working and didn't realize how late it was. You all want pizza for dinner?"

"Yes!" Ava and Waverly shouted.

Ava's mum picked up her phone, then turned to Libby.

"Good with you, too?" she asked. "You're not gluten-free, vegan, paleo- or lactose intolerant, are you?"

Libby stared at her. What in the world was she talking about? "No," she finally answered. "Pizza sounds good."

And it was. Very good. Extremely good. "More, please!" she said after she had gobbled up her first slice. She ate four pieces in all. It was crispy, saucy, cheesy deliciousness. It was deceptively simple-looking, but it was the perfect combination of comforting flavours. *Mission 2, Wishworld Observation #7: Everyone must try pizza!*

Ava's mum was reaching for another slice when she gasped. She looked at her watch. "Oops, time to go pick up Jasper!" she cried. "Be back soon, girls!"

Libby looked at Ava.

"My annoying little brother," she explained.

The girls had finished cleaning up and Ava was turning on the dishwasher (another odd Wishling invention) when a young male Wishling about a year or two younger than Ava swaggered into the kitchen. He had red hair and a smirk on his freckled face. Libby eyed him warily. He flipped open the lid of the pizza box and grabbed a slice. "Good thing you saved me some, Ava," he said.

"Can't you say hello, Jasper?" Ava asked.

"Hello, Jasper," he said with a smirk.

Ava rolled her eyes. "Brothers," she said.

Waverly placed a sheaf of papers in front of Ava. "So," she said, "I took the liberty of jotting down some ideas for you."

Ava looked at her quizzically. "You ... um ... wrote my speech for me?" she asked.

"Just as a starting point, of course," said Waverly, raising a hand as if to deflect criticism.

Ava picked up the papers and studied them. She looked up. "It looks like you wrote the whole thing."

"It's just some ideas," Waverly protested.

Ava cleared her throat and began. "'Good afternoon, Principal Lefkon, Vice Principal Bergen, teachers, fellow classmates,'" she read. "'My name is Ava Cunningham, and I am running for class president. This is a challenge that I accept both solemnly and wholeheartedly. There are some who think that the school government is a laughing matter.'" There Ava frowned. "'Well, I assure you....'" She lost her place for a moment. "'I assure you', " she repeated, "'that I am ready to accept this responsibility with the gravity that it commands. I intend to lead my fellow students in a manner becoming of a –'"

"It's good," interrupted Jasper.

Waverly put her hands on her hips and smiled.

"It is?" said Libby. She wasn't so sure about that.

"Yeah," answered Jasper. "It's good if you want your audience to die of boredom!"

Libby let out a strangled laugh. She had to agree.

"Jasper!" Waverly snapped huffily. "Mind your own business!"

"Here's what you should say," said Jasper. He climbed up on a kitchen stool, put one hand over his heart and pointed a finger in the air. "I am Ava Cunningham," he said in a high, squeaky voice that sounded nothing it all like Ava's low, pleasant voice. "And you should vote for me for president because I am so kind and generous. In fact, I am so very generous that when I was eight years old, I once shared something very special with my amazing little brother. I gave him a terrible case of the itchiest ..."

Ava's eyes opened wide. She obviously knew exactly what was coming next. The look on her face was one of pure panic. "I wish you would stop talking!" she shouted. Another wish from her Wisher! Libby immediately hopped into action. *Shut up, shut up, shut up,* she chanted in her head, staring at Jasper.

"... scratchiest case of head li–"

All of a sudden Jasper fell silent. His mouth opened and closed but nothing came out. His eyes nearly bulged out of his head.

Ava looked relieved. "Very funny, Jasper," she said. "Now get out of here, please."

Jasper ran out of the room, panic-stricken. And Libby probably waited a little longer than she should have to reverse the wish. But she eventually did.

Libby yawned loudly. She was exhausted.

"Keeping you up, I see," said Waverly. "Now let's get back to the speech."

Ava gathered up the notes and took a deep breath. She looked at Waverly. "So I was thinking of maybe starting with a joke, to loosen up the audience. Have you ever heard this one?" She smiled. "What do you call cheese that isn't yours?"

"What?" asked Libby.

"Nacho cheese!" said Ava. "Get it?"

Libby laughed as if she understood, though she really didn't.

Ava smiled. "Then I could go into my campaign promise about improving the school lunch menu selections. What do you think?"

Waverly, looking slightly annoyed, shook her head. "Stick to your message, Ava," she said. "You are the serious candidate. Leave the jokes to bubble gum girl."

"Don't you mean *your* message?" Libby thought she heard Ava mutter. But she wasn't exactly sure, and then Ava shrugged and said, "Whatever you think is best," so Libby let it go.

Several hours and one serious election speech later, the girls were lying in Ava's room. Ava was on the floor in a sleeping bag, as she had graciously given her guests her large bed to sleep in. Ava had recited the speech several times, until Waverly was satisfied. Libby was feeling confident that everything was under control.

"Are you sure I shouldn't start with a joke?" Ava asked. "It just feels right, like it's going to get their attention."

Waverly yawned. "You're not running to be class clown," she said. "You're running to be class president."

Ava rolled over. "Fine," she said. She stared at Libby for a moment. "I love your hair, Libby. That pink streak is so cool." She smiled sleepily. "I wish I had pink hair."

Libby's eyes opened wide. Pink hair! How many wishes could one Wisher make! This was getting ridiculous. Still, she closed her eyes and concentrated. But she was so very tired....

Starf! Libby sat up suddenly as a blaring ringing noise shocked her out of a deep sleep. It took a starmin to identify the obnoxious sound. Wishworld alarms were loud and annoying. Libby much preferred the gentle Starland alarm: your bed was gently vibrated until you got out of it. It was a very pleasant way to wake up. This, not so much. What a jarring way to start your day. Plus, they were getting up extra early to hang up the new posters. The election was the next day.

Ava was the first to get up. She unzipped her sleeping bag, stood up, and stumbled to the bathroom. Libby heard the click as the light was switched on. And then the scream.

Libby and Waverly ran to the bathroom. Libby threw open the door. Ava was staring at herself in the mirror. Her hair was half brown, half pink. Libby realized she must have fallen asleep in the middle of her wish. *Oops.*

Waverly shook her head. "Oh, no ... no, no, no, no," she said. "No," she added for good measure.

Ava smiled at her reflection. "It's actually pretty cool," she said. "But how in the world...."

"We have to fix this before the election!" said Waverly frantically. "This is not the hair of a serious presidential candidate!"

Libby thought fast. "It's just temporary," she said. "Don't worry. It will come out in the shower."

"It better," said Waverly warningly.

"It will," said Libby. "I guarantee it." And she thought, *Mission 2, Wishworld Observation #8: Sometimes wishes are wishes. But then again, sometimes they aren't. Be careful out there; it's hard to tell the difference.*

Ava came out of the bathroom, towel-drying her back-to-normal hair. Libby went in next, and she found that Ava had left for her a change of clothes, a tube of something minty called toothpaste and a brand-new instrument, still in its package – a toothbrush.

Libby stood in the bathroom, staring at the toothbrush. She stuck it in her mouth and moved it around. She couldn't be entirely sure she was doing it correctly. Was it up and down or side to side? She missed her toothlight.

Libby had been deliberately avoiding mirrors since she had arrived, knowing she would be horrified by her dull Wishling appearance. And she was. She gasped at her plain brown hair, her flat-looking skin. What she wouldn't give for a little sparkle. She was feeling so tired, too, which made her look extra un-sparkly, in her opinion. Suddenly, she remembered her Mirror Mantra.

Libby stared at her reflection and spoke the words: "It's all in the balance. Glimmer and shine."

She grinned as her appearance was suddenly transformed and she looked as she did on Starland. Her eyes lit up and she touched the mirror. How she missed her long, flowing pink hair and glimmery skin! How did Wishlings deal with being so boring and uninspiring all the time?

The next morning, Libby's Mirror Mantra had given her the burst of confidence and energy she needed. When they arrived at school, she bustled around the hallway, wanting to get the posters up before the rest of the students began trickling in. They had an election to win. And the next day she would have some wish energy (a lot of it, she hoped) to collect. She glanced down at her Wish Pendant, dangling from her neck. *Starf!* Her wish energy was getting low. Luckily, everything was falling into place. Libby was confident that she wouldn't need her special talent to make this wish come true.

CHAPTER
9

"This will all be over by tomorrow afternoon," said Ava as she and Libby climbed the stairs together on the way to class after they had hung all the posters. "Thank goodness."

"You don't sound all that excited," Libby said.

Ava shrugged.

"So what made you decide to run for president?" Libby asked.

"It happened by accident," Ava said with a sigh. "No one was running, and the principal made an announcement at assembly one morning urging students to throw their hats into the ring."

Libby's eyes widened. What did tossing your hat have to do with an election?

"That's exactly what she said," Ava continued. "And I was wearing a hat, so of course I tossed it up onto the stage as a joke, and then the next thing I knew, Sammy Decker nominated me right then and there. And then no one else wanted to run and the principal kept saying that someone else had to run against me, they couldn't just give it to me, so I talked Kristie into running, too. We figured that one of us would win and then the other person would help them out. It didn't matter who won to us. We thought it would be fun."

Libby considered this. "That's interesting. But then things changed, obviously."

"This girl named Holly volunteered to be Kristie's campaign manager. And then little by little things started getting competitive. Fancy posters. Free candy if you promised to vote for her. Then Kristie got really busy after school all the time and couldn't spend time with me. Then Waverly volunteered to help me, and then, before I knew it, Kristie and I stopped talking. It was so weird."

"That is weird," Libby nodded. "So what happens tomorrow afternoon?"

"Tomorrow afternoon the whole school comes to the auditorium to hear our speeches," Ava said. "Then everyone votes. They count up the ballots, and the one of us with the most votes wins."

And then you *win*, Libby thought. *One more day and then you win.*

"I still don't know why the lunch lady freaked out," said Waverly as they headed out of the cafeteria that afternoon. "She just started yelling about chicken fingers out of the blue. It was so bizarre."

Libby shrugged tiredly. She had a pretty good idea about what had happened. She had discovered her special talent – the ability to turn one Wishling object into another. In line, as they held their trays, she had overheard Ava softly saying, "I wish that they would serve chicken fingers today." And before Libby knew it, she had transformed a tray of turkey sliders into chicken fingers. (Whatever those were, she didn't want to know!) Libby couldn't help herself. She hadn't realized that it would completely freak the lunch lady out. *No more little wishes!* Libby thought. *Concentrate on the big wish. You're almost done.* She stole a glance at the Countdown Clock. She was right on target for the election the next day. She just needed to focus.

"Imagine mixing up sliders and chicken fingers," said Waverly. "So strange." The three girls had finished their lunches quickly and left the cafeteria early. They walked down the hall, turned a corner and headed towards their classroom. They all gasped at the same time. The hallway was lined with the posters they had taped up that morning. But now each picture had a large moustache drawn on Ava's serious face! They looked so funny that Libby almost burst out laughing. But a glance at Ava's confused expression and Waverly's furious one forced her to clap her mouth shut.

"I can't believe it!" said Ava. "Who would have done such a thing?"

"I can believe it," said Waverly, crossing her arms tightly. "Politics is a dirty business. It's a stupid joke that has Kristie and Holly written all over it. Well, now we have no choice. We have to retaliate." She thought for a moment and nodded. "We have to pop all of the balloons on their posters."

"Waverly!" said Ava. "We can't do that!" She looked down at the floor, her expression sad. "I just can't believe that Kristie would do that to me." She shook her head. "I can't believe it's come to this."

"Believe it," said Waverly. "That's politics."

Libby thought fast. "Listen," she said. "You have to look at both sides. Sure, maybe Kristie did draw moustaches on all of Ava's posters. If so, that's not right. But if she did and Ava retaliates, she's sinking to her level. She could get caught and be disqualified. Or people could get turned off by the bad behaviour and they won't know who to vote for. Or maybe they don't vote at all. Nobody wins."

Waverly opened her mouth to speak, but Libby held up her hand.

"And just suppose Kristie *didn't* do it. It's completely possible that some random kid grabbed a pen and decided to be artistic." She smiled. "The artist didn't sign his or her work, so we'll never know."

"Well, we can't leave them up," wailed Waverly. "She'll be the laughing stock of the school!" She stomped over to one of the posters. "Fine," she spat out. "We'll just take them down."

"Wait!" Libby cried. She thought for a moment, then smiled. "I have the perfect idea."

She held out her hand. "Do either of you have one of those...." She searched her brain for the Wishling word. "One of those thick black writing utensils?"

The girls stared at her. "Do you mean a pen?" Ava asked, looking at her oddly.

That's what it's called! she thought, making a mental note. "Yes, one of those," said Libby.

Ava fished around in her bag and pulled out a black-capped pen. "Here you go," she said.

Libby marched over to the first poster and fixed it. It was awkward – and enjoyable – to write on paper instead of in the air on a holo-notebook.

When Ava saw what Libby had done, she laughed and laughed. "Oh Libby, it's perfect!" she chortled. "Just my style!"

Waverly shook her head. "I think it's silly," she said. She walked up to the poster and looked again. "Yup, I hate it," she said.

"Get over it," said Libby saucily. "Everyone is going to love it. Trust me."

Was she right? Libby watched, holding her breath, as the end-of-lunch bell rang and students started spilling out of the cafeteria. The first group stopped short in front of one of the posters. After a moment they all began pointing and laughing.

"That's awesome!"

"So funny!"

"Hysterical!"

Libby and Ava had gone up and down the hallway drawing speech balloons on each poster next to Ava's moustachioed face. Then they had carefully written: I MOUSTACHE YOU TO VOTE FOR ME! in the balloons.

Ava's eyes were shining. "Everyone's laughing. They think it's funny. It's exactly what I wanted in the first place!" she said. "Thank you, Libby!"

"You're welcome," said Libby.

CHAPTER
10

Libby had one more trick up her sleeve to make sure that Ava's wish came true. She wanted to surprise Ava and Waverly. Ava because she knew she'd be delighted and Waverly because she would try to stop her. Luckily, she had a bit of wish energy left, and hopefully there was enough. "Meet me on the front steps tomorrow morning for a cool surprise," Libby told Ava. She didn't ask to sleep over that night, because she was planning to sleep on the school roof in her special Star Darlings tent. She could work her Starling magic in the privacy of her own invisible tent. And she could also sleep in. A Star Darling, especially a tired one, needed her rest.

The next morning Libby stored her energy tent back in her Star-Zap, packed up her surprise, and waited for Ava on the steps. She made sure her back was turned as Ava approached her.

"Hey, Libby," said Ava, tapping her shoulder.

Libby turned around, and Ava shrieked with laughter. Libby twirled the end of her large fake moustache and waggled her eyebrows. "I moustache you to wear one of these!" she said. The night before, she had used her special talent of transformation to change hundreds of twigs she had collected after school into stick-on moustaches. She was quite exhausted. Her Wish Pendant was spent. She placed a moustache under Ava's nose. "Here," she said, handing Ava a full shopping bag. "Moustaches for everyone!"

Ava grinned, though it was hard to see under the moustache. "This is the most awesome thing ever. Thank you!" She smiled ruefully. "Waverly is going to hate this, you know."

"Don't I know it," said Libby.

Libby stood backstage, observing from a distance. She stole a glance at her Countdown Clock. It was only a matter of starmins now. Ava and Kristie would give their speeches, and the students would fill out their ballots and drop them into ballot boxes on their way out of the auditorium. It didn't have to be a landslide. If Ava got just one vote more than Kristie, her wish would come true. And Libby was sure that was going to happen.

Suddenly, Libby felt so exhausted she had to sit down, sinking onto a cardboard box that stood nearby. The top collapsed and she sat there uncomfortably, her feet dangling above the floor and her bottom firmly wedged inside. Now that was awkward.

Waverly bustled by, then grabbed Libby's hand and pulled her to her feet. "This is no time to relax," she scolded. "We have an election to win!" She clapped her hands together. "Now where's Ava?" she asked. Libby pointed Ava out and Waverly headed in her direction.

Libby walked to the edge of the stage and peeked out from behind the heavy red stage curtain. Kristie was in the middle of her speech. She was making a lot of jokes and the audience was laughing at most of them. That was worrisome. But almost everyone in the audience was sporting a fake moustache. That was a good sign. Things were looking great. Really great.

A familiar voice came from behind her. "Excuse me."

Libby had a sinking feeling in her stomach as she turned around. As she had feared, it was Sage –

a Wishling version of her, with light brown hair and Wishling clothing.

"Wh-wh-what are you doing here?" Libby asked, bewildered. "I really don't think I need any help. It's all falling into place."

"Hey, what's that on your face?"

Libby reached up. "Oh, it's a moustache. Want one?" She pulled one out of her pocket, peeled off its backing, and put it under Sage's nose.

"Um, thanks," said Sage, making a funny face. "So back to business. Lady Stella seems to think that something's not quite right with your mission. Look at your pendant, it's totally empty!" She looked closely at Libby. "Plus, are you tired?"

"Very," Libby admitted. "But I think that's because I was granting these silly little wishes my Wisher was making. It took a lot out of me. The main wish is totally under control." She pointed out to the audience. "And it's just about to come true."

"I wouldn't be so sure about that," said Sage. "There's got to be something else going on. Let's think. Are you absolutely certain that you identified the correct Wisher?"

"Absolutely," said Libby firmly. "My Wish Pendant was glowing, no question about it."

"Then it must be the wish that's wrong," Sage said.

"Impossible," said Libby. Her eyes swept the backstage area. Ava stood in the wings with Waverly. It looked like she was getting a pep talk. But then Libby took a closer look. She suddenly realized that Ava was not paying attention. She was staring at Kristie. And she didn't look nervous, or competitive, or even particularly interested in what Kristie was saying. She was smiling, but there was a look of sadness in her eyes. And suddenly everything made perfect sense.

"You're right," she told Sage. "I messed up." But how was she going to fix this? She looked at Sage, panic stricken. "I'm not sure what to do," she told her. Should she stop the election? Try to get the two girls to talk to each other? Grab the microphone and talk to both of them? Sage held out her hands. "Let's say your Mirror Mantra together," she said. "It will help you decide." The two girls held hands. "It's all in the balance. Glimmer and shine," they said together. A feeling of pure peace flowed through Libby. Her jumbled thoughts were gone. And suddenly she knew exactly what to do.

"Good luck!" said Sage.

Libby walked over to Ava and Waverly.

Waverly looked at Libby. "I don't know what to do," she said. "She needs to get out there and give the speech of her life. And it's like she couldn't care less. Will you see what you can do?"

"I will," said Libby. "Just give us a minute." She stared at Waverly, who was lingering to eavesdrop. "A little privacy?" she asked.

Waverly looked uncertain, but she did as she was asked.

Ava looked at Libby. "There's nothing to say. I don't need a pep talk. I'll be fine." She sighed deeply.

Libby put her hand on Ava's shoulder. "I got it wrong," she said. "When we first met, you said you wished for something. I assumed you wished that you would win the election. But what you wished for was that you could win your best friend back. Is that right?"

Ava nodded, looking at the floor. "That's right."

"Why didn't you say anything?" asked Libby sadly.

"It just seemed pointless," Ava said. "And Waverly was working so hard, and then you joined in. You guys had done so much, and I just felt bad. I felt like I had to see it through. But I don't care about this stupid election. I just want my best friend back."

Libby's heart sank. How in the world was she going to fix this?

"There's no time," she said. "You have this speech to make and...." Suddenly, Libby was inspired. "Hand me your speech," she said. "And make it snappy." She glanced at her Countdown Clock. "We're almost out of time."

Ava handed it over. "What are you doing?" she asked.

"Turn around," Libby instructed. Using Ava's back as a makeshift desk, she scribbled some words on the paper. "Hope you can read my handwriting," she said.

She handed the paper back to Ava, who looked panicked.

Kristie finished her speech to applause and cheers.

The principal walked over to the microphone. "And now please put your hands together for presidential candidate Ava Cunningham!" she said.

"You can do it," said Libby. "You can make your wish come true. It's a wish from the heart. Your heart."

Ava stumbled onto the stage. The audience was silent. She slowly made her way to the podium. Libby held her breath as Ava blinked for a moment at the large audience.

"Speech!" someone called out. A couple of students laughed.

Ava looked down and scanned the paper. And then she began to speak. "Hi, everyone, my name is Ava Cunningham. You've probably seen my posters around school, asking you to vote for me. I've shaken many of your hands in the hallway, telling you that I am the best candidate for this job. And here," she held up the paper, "I have a carefully written speech about all the things I'll do as class president, and how you should vote for me instead of Kristie. But I'm not going to read it."

Waverly stomped over to Libby. "Are you kidding me?" she said furiously. "What kind of pep talk did you give her?"

Libby held up a hand. Waverly crossed her arms tightly, her mouth set in a grim line.

"I'm here to talk about something else," Ava continued. "I'm here today to tell you about someone who has a great sense of humour and really cares about this school. Someone who will be the best president you guys could want. I used to call her my very best friend. And her name is Kristie Chang."

Waverly shook her head. "What a disaster!" she said.

The crowd began to murmur. "That's right," said Ava. "I am dropping out of the race. It cost me the thing that was most important to me. So please vote for my very best friend, Kristie Chang, for class president!"

There was a stunned silence.

Libby stepped onstage. And then she began to clap. At first she was the only one. But then, one by one, the students started to applaud, until the whole school, faculty included, were on their feet, cheering for Ava.

A hush fell over the crowd. Kristie was making her way onstage. She stepped up to the microphone. "In the campaign I also lost sight of what's most important. I miss you, Ava. If it's okay with the student council, I propose that we be co-presidents. No election needed!"

Ava looked shocked. Then her face broke into a huge smile, and she hugged Kristie. The audience erupted into cheers.

Libby rushed onstage and handed the young female Wishlings matching moustaches. They put them on and waved at the audience, who burst into laughter.

"I moustache you to be my best friend again," Libby heard Ava say to Kristie.

Kristie nodded. "Of course," she said. "I really missed you." The crowd cheered.

"Now watch," said Sage, appearing at Libby's side. Rainbow light energy began to flow from Ava, dancing across the stage in a joyful stream as it was absorbed into Libby's Wish Pendant. It was amazingly breathtaking. Libby felt sorry that she and Sage were the only two who could see it.

"I'm sorry, Libby, but it's time to say goodbye," Sage said.

Libby frowned. She had really grown to like Ava.

She was proud that she had helped bring two friends back together, and she wanted to enjoy the moment for a bit longer. But the mission was a success, her identity was still a secret, and the wish energy had been collected. It was time to go home.

Libby found Ava in the auditorium happily accepting congratulations from students and teachers alike. Ava threw her arms around Libby. "Thanks so much for helping me," she said. "Nice moustache."

"Thanks," said Libby, twirling the end. "I think it suits me. And it was my pleasure." She took a deep breath. "I don't know how to tell you this, but I've got to go."

"I wish ... " said Ava. Libby cringed for a moment. "I wish you didn't have to go. But something is telling me that it's important."

Libby reached forward and hugged her tightly. "You're right," she whispered. When the two broke from their embrace, Ava gave Libby a polite smile, as if Libby was just another supporter wishing her well. "Thank you," she said. "I promise to be a good co-president."

"I'm sure you'll be the best," said Libby.

Epilogue

"Star salutations," Libby told Sage as they made their way across campus back on Starland. "I couldn't have done it without you."

"No problem," said Sage. "I'm glad I could help."

As the moving pavement travelled past Halo Hall, the two girls noticed a crowd of students outside, grouped around the holo-announcement board. Sage looked at Libby. "Do you think it could be the band results?" she asked.

"Could be," said Libby. "Let's go see." They stepped off the moving pavement and headed over to see what was going on.

They joined the crowd and waited patiently so they could take a peek. A student shoved her way back through the crowd with an exasperated look on her face. "Whatever," she said scornfully. "It's all those Star Dippers. They should just call it Stupidrock."

Libby and Sage looked at each other. Could it be true? When they got to the front of the line, they saw the list:

THE STAR DARLINGS
LEAD SINGER: LEONA
GUITAR: SAGE
BASS: VEGA
DRUMS: SCARLET
KEYTAR: LIBBY

"Can you believe it?" someone asked behind them. Libby turned around. It was Leona. She had a big grin on her face. "An all-Star Darling band. Chosen by the Ranker as the best possible combination of musicians. Who would have thought?"

Then she frowned. "I'm not sure about the name, though. I was thinking of something snappier."

"Like what?" asked Sage.

"Like Leona and the Luminaries," suggested Leona.

Libby laughed. "It's fine just as it is," she told her. Libby grinned. This was exciting news on top of her successful mission. It was a good group. Leona, well, she could be a handful. But Libby was sure the other girls, especially Scarlet, would help balance out Leona's extra-large personality. Libby practically skipped all the way to her room.

The door slid open, and the first thing Libby saw was the flowers. Oddly enough, they hadn't faded. They were actually just as fresh-looking as the day the girls had got them. The smell, if anything, had got even stronger.

"You're back!" cried Gemma, looking up from her holo-book. "Was your mission a success?"

"It was," said Libby. "But it had its setbacks. I suppose I'll be in the starlight tomorrow in class."

"Probably," agreed Gemma, perhaps a little too quickly. "So the band results are in," she told Libby.

"I just saw them," Libby replied. "I'm sorry."

Gemma cocked her head at Libby. "Are you?"

Libby surprised herself by answering truthfully. "I – I don't know."

Gemma shook her head. "I thought so. You know, we haven't been getting along at all, and it makes me so sad. But lately I just find you so ... so...."

"Annoying?" offered Libby.

"Yes, that's exactly it. Annoying!"

"Me too!" cried Libby. The girls looked at each other,

momentarily glad to have something in common again. But as the reality of what it was sank in, their faces fell.

Just then their Star-Zaps went off. Libby felt relieved. It wasn't easy to tell the person you lived with that her very presence irritated you. Or to hear it, come to think of it. She frowned. She knew why Gemma was annoying, but why in the world was Gemma annoyed by her?

Everyone rose to their feet as Libby entered Lady Stella's office. "Libby!" the headmistress cried. "Congratulations on a job well done!"

Libby grinned as everyone burst into applause.

"Star salutations," she said as the girls hugged her and clapped her on the back. She basked in the admiration of her fellow Star Darlings. "It wasn't easy. But it's over!"

"I have something for you," said Lady Stella, reaching toward her desk drawer. But then her Star-Zap buzzed. She reached into the pocket of her midnight-blue tunic and pulled it out. Libby watched as she read a message. A look of shock, followed by severe dismay, crossed the headmistress's face. Libby felt panicked.

"Excuse me," Lady Stella said, looking flustered. She left the room abruptly, leaving the door ajar.

Everyone stopped talking. They could hear Lady Stella speaking in low tones outside the door. Leona silently crept to the door and started listening. Even though they knew it was wrong, no one stopped her.

Leona listened intently, then turned to the group. "She said, 'How on Starland could this happen?'" she reported in a whisper.

Libby bit her lip. Tessa and Gemma put their arms around each other. Cassie wrung her hands.

"I can't hear what the other person is saying. Wait. Lady Stella is talking again." Leona paused. "She said, 'What a terrible mistake.'"

Libby felt her heart sink. There must have been a problem with her mission. She looked down at her Wish Pendant. It looked like it was full. What could be wrong?

Leona listened again. "She said, 'How can we fix this?'"

Some of the Star Darlings began to whisper among themselves. "Shhhhhhh!" commanded Leona. She strained to hear. "Oh, no," she said.

"What is it? What is it?" Gemma cried.

Leona turned to the girls with tears in her eyes. She could hardly get the words out. "She said ... she said...."

"Spit it out, Leona," said Astra. "You're killing us!"

"She said, 'How in the world am I going to tell her that she isn't really a Star Darling?'"

There was a collective gasp. Libby couldn't even look at the other girls. Did this mean one of them was an imposter? Libby didn't want to see the furtive looks in her classmates' eyes as they glanced at one another, each hoping it wasn't herself, wishing that someone else would receive the terrible news. It was an awful, selfish, difficult-to-deal-with feeling.

The door slid open. Leona jumped back. Everyone stared at the floor. Lady Stella stepped into the room, her face ashen. She walked to the middle of the room and simply stood there, her head bowed.

Finally, she spoke. "Girls, I just received some terrible, shocking news." Her eyes were wet and she wrung her hands. "Something very unexpected has come up. I don't even know how to begin," she sighed. "I'm going to have to ask you all to leave. Libby, I'm sorry. We will have to postpone your Wish Orb presentation."

The girls began to file out of the room. Libby fell into place at the end of the line. The only sound was their feet shuffling across the carpet.

Lady Stella spoke up. "Everyone except for ... Scarlet."

Scarlet stopped in her tracks, her expression frozen. Libby didn't think she would forget that sad, resigned, fearful look for as long as she lived.

"Scarlet, we need to talk," Lady Stella said gently. "I'm afraid I have some bad news."

And then Libby didn't hear any more, because the door slid shut behind her with a loud click.

Glossary

Bad Wish Orbs: Orbs that are a result of bad or selfish wishes made on Wishworld, these grow dark and warped and are quickly sent to the Negative Energy Facility.

Band shell: A covered stage located in the Star Quad.

Bitterball: This fruit is inedible straight off the vine, but can be made into tasty preserves by adding sweetener.

Bloombug: Purple-and-pink-spotted bug that goes wild during the full moon in warm weather.

Blushbelle: A pink flower with a sweetly spicy scent. Libby's favourite flower.

Bot-Bot: A Starland robot. There are Bot-Bot guards, waiters, deliverers and guides on Starland.

Bright Day: The date a Starling is born, celebrated each year like Wishling birthdays.

Calaka: A round yellow vegetable often used in salads or on sandwiches.

Celestial Café: Starling Academy's outstanding cafeteria.

Chatterburst: An orange flower that smells like orange-and-vanilla ice pops. Gemma's favourite flower.

Cocomoon: A sweet and creamy fruit with an iridescent glow.

Cosmic Transporter: The moving pavement system that transports students through dorms and across the Starling Academy campus.

Countdown Clock: A timing device on a Starling's Star-Zap; it lets them know how much time is left on a Wish Mission, which coincides with when the Wish Orb will fade.

Crystal Mountains: The most beautiful mountains on Starland, they are located across the lake from Starling Academy.

Cyber Journal: Where the Star Darlings record their Wishworld observations.

Cycle of Life: A Starling's lifespan. When a Starling dies, they are said to have "completed their Cycle of Life".

first stars: Starlings often call "first stars" when they want to go first at something. Akin to the Wishling expression "I call first dibs".

Flash Vertical Mover: A mode of transport similar to a Wishling lift, only superfast.

Flutterfocus: A Starland creature similar to a Wishworld butterfly with illuminated wings.

Galliope: A Starland creature similar to a sparkly Wishworld horse.

Glamora-ora: A luxury holiday destination with crystal-pink waters and soft purple sands.

Glimmerchips: A popular snack food, they are thin, crispy and salty. Similar to Wishworld crisps, but sparkly and even more delicious.

Glion: A gentle Starland creature similar in appearance to a Wishworld lion, but with a multicoloured glowing mane.

Glorange: A glowing orange fruit, its juice is often enjoyed at breakfast time.

Goldenella tree: Its flowers bloom non-stop for a week and pop off the branches like popcorn.

Good Wish Orbs: Orbs that are the result of positive wishes made on Wishworld. They are planted in Wish-Houses.

Googlehorn: An unwieldy silver instrument with three separate horns, it has a deep bass sound.

Go supernova: When a Starling is said to "go supernova", they get really angry.

Halo Hall: The building where Starling Academy classes are held.

Holo-announcement board: An announcement board that projects announcements into the air. There are also *holo-billboards*, *holo-books*, *holo-cards*, *holo-communications*, *holo-flyers* and *holo-pictures* – anything that would be made of paper on Wishworld is a hologram on Starland.

Hydrong: Equivalent of a Wishworld hundred.

Illumination Library: The impressive library at Starling Academy.

Impossible Wish Orbs: Orbs that are a result of wishes made on Wishworld that are beyond the power of Starlings to grant.

Isle of Misera: A barren, rocky island off the coast of New Prism.

Jellyjooble: A small, round pink candy that is very sweet.

Lightfall: The time of day when the sun begins to set and everything on Starland glows its brightest.

Light Leader: The head of the Starling Academy student government.

Lightning Lounge: The place where students relax and socialize.

Little Dipper Dormitory: Where first- and second-year students live.

Lolofruit: A large round fruit with a thick skin and juicy, aromatic flesh.

Melodeon: A Starling instrument similar to a tiny accordion that produces a very high-pitched sound.

Mirror Mantra: A saying specific to each Star Darling that when recited gives her (and her Wisher) reassurance and strength. When a Starling recites her Mirror Mantra while looking in a mirror, she will see her true appearance reflected.

New Prism: This casual and easygoing port city is Scarlet's hometown.

Pluckalong: A small three-stringed instrument, it is played with the fingers. It has a round wooden body and a short neck.

Radiant Hills: An exclusive community in Starland City, where Libby's family lives.

Radiant Recreation Centre: Starling Academy's state-of-the-art fitness and sports centre.

Ranker: A small machine that judges competitions and picks the winners. Its fair program eliminates favouritism.

Safety starglasses: Worn by Starlings to protect their eyes when in close proximity to a shooting star.

Shooting stars: Speeding stars that Starlings can latch on to and ride to Wishworld.

Solar Springs: A hilly small town in the countryside where Tessa and Gemma are from.

Sparkle juice: An effervescent and refreshing beverage, often enjoyed over ice.

Starberry: Large bright-red fruits that grow in clusters.

Starcake: A Starling breakfast item, similar to a star-shaped Wishworld pancake.

Starcar: The primary mode of transport for most Starlings.

These ultrasafe vehicles drive themselves on cushions of wish energy.

Star Caves: The caverns underneath Starling Academy where the Star Darlings' secret Wish-Cavern is located.

Starf: A Starling expression of dismay.

Starflooty: A wind instrument with star-shaped holes.

Starkin: The Starling word for siblings.

Starkudos: A Starling expression of praise.

Starland: The irregularly shaped world where Starlings live, veiled by a bright yellow glow that, from a distance, makes it look like a star.

Starland City: The largest city on Starland, also its capital. Sage, Libby and Adora's hometown.

Starlight: When all eyes are on a Starling, they are said to be "in the starlight".

Starling Academy: The most prestigious all-girl four-year boarding school for wish granting on Starland.

Starlings: The glowing beings with sparkly skin that live on Starland.

Starling's Surprise, The: A classic children's book, beloved by many. It tells the tale of a young female Starling and her adventures with a talking glion.

Starmin: Sixty starsecs (or seconds) on Starland, the equivalent of a Wishworld minute.

Star Preparatory: Similar to Starling Academy, this is the all-boys school located across Luminous Lake.

Star Quad: The central outdoor part of the Starling Academy campus.

Star salutations: A Starling expression of thanks.

Starsec: Brief period of time, similar to a Wishworld second.

Star shakers: Clear star-shaped musical instruments with handles, which are filled with crystals that produce a delicate tinkling sound when shaken.

Star Wranglers: Starlings whose job is to lasso a shooting star, to transport Starlings to Wishworld.

Star-Zap: The ultimate smartphone that Starlings use for all communications. It has myriad features.

Student Manual: A holo-book that contains all the rules and regulations of Starling Academy.

Supernova Island: An exclusive holiday destination with fine restaurants, fancy shops and stunning views from its mountainous peaks.

Time of Letting Go: One of the four seasons on Starland. It falls between the warmest season and the coldest, and is similar to autumn on Wishworld.

Time of Lumiere: The warmest season on Starland, similar to summer on Wishworld.

Time of New Beginnings: Similar to spring on Wishworld, this is the season that follows the coldest time of the year; it's when plants and trees come into bloom.

Time of Shadows: The coldest season of the year on Starland, similar to winter on Wishworld.

Timpanpipe: An ancient brass instrument, it makes a scratchy, whistly sound.

Tinsel toast: Bread heated and sprinkled with ground tinsel, a sweet, aromatic, glittery plant.

Toothlight: A high-tech gadget that Starlings use to clean their teeth.

Wish Blossom: The bloom that appears from a Wish Orb after its wish is granted.

Wish energy: The positive energy that is released when a wish is granted. Wish energy powers everything on Starland.

Wish energy manipulation: The ability to mentally harness wish energy to perform physical acts like turning off lights, closing doors, etc.

Wisher: The Wishling who has made the wish that is being granted.

Wish-House: The place where Wish Orbs are planted and cared for until they sparkle. Once the orb's wish is granted, it becomes a Wish Blossom.

Wishlings: The inhabitants of Wishworld.

Wish Mission: The task Starlings undertake when they travel to Wishworld to help grant a wish.

Wish Orb: The form a wish takes on Wishworld before travelling to Starland. It will grow and sparkle when it's time to grant the wish.

Wish Pendant: A gadget that absorbs and transports wish energy, helps Starlings locate their Wishers, and changes their appearance. Each Wish Pendant holds a different special power for its Star Darling.

Wish-Watcher: Starlings whose job it is to observe the Good Wish Orbs until they glow, indicating that they are ready to be granted.

Wishworld: The planet that Starland relies on for wish energy. The beings on Wishworld know it by another name – Earth.

Wishworld Outfit Selector: A program on each Star-Zap that accesses Wishworld fashions for Starlings to wear to blend in.

Wishworld Surveillance Deck: Located high above the campus, it is where Starling Academy students go to observe Wishlings through high-powered telescopes.

Zing: A traditional Starling breakfast drink, it can be enjoyed hot or iced.

Zoomberry: Small, sweetly tart berries that grow in abundance on Starland.

Acknowledgements

It is impossible to list all of our gratitude, but we will try.

Our most precious gift and greatest teacher, Halo; we love you more than there are stars in the sky ... punashaku. To the rest of our crazy, awesome, unique tribe – thank you for teaching us to go for our dreams. Integrity. Strength. Love. Foundation. Family. Grateful. Mimi Muldoon – from your star doodling to naming our Star Darlings, your artistry, unconditional love and inspiration is infinite. Didi Muldoon – your belief and support in us is only matched by your fierce protection and massive-hearted guidance. Gail. Queen G. Your business sense and witchy wisdom are legendary. Frank – you are missed and we know you are watching over us all. Along with Tutu, Nana and Deda, who are always present, gently guiding us in spirit. To our colourful, totally genius and bananas siblings – Patrick, Moon, Diva and Dweezil – there is more creativity and humour in those four names than most people experience in a lifetime. Blessed. To our magical nieces – Mathilda, Zola, Ceylon and Mia – the Star Darlings adore you and so do we. Our witchy cuzzie fairy godmothers – Ane and Gina. Our fairy fashion godfather, Paris. Teeta and Freddy – we love you all so much. And our four-legged fur babies – Sandwich, Luna, Figgy and Pinky Star.

The incredible Barry Waldo. Our SD partner. Sent to us from above in perfect timing. Your expertise and friendship are beyond words. We love you and Gary to the moon and back. Long live the manifestation room!

Catherine Daly – the stars shone brightly upon us the day we aligned with you. Your talent and inspiration are otherworldly; our appreciation cannot be expressed in words. Many heartfelt hugs for you and the adorable Oonagh.

To our beloved Disney family. Thank you for believing in us. Wendy Lefkon, our master guide and friend through this entire journey. Stephanie Lurie, for being the first to believe in Star Darlings. Suzanne Murphy, who helped every step of the way. Jeanne Mosure, we fell in love with you the first time we met and Star Darlings wouldn't be what it is without you. Andrew Sugarman, thank you so much for all your support.

Our team ... Devon (pony pants) and our Monsterfoot crew – so grateful. Richard Scheltinga – our angel and protector. Chris Abramson – thank you! Special appreciation to Richard Thompson, John LaViolette, Swanna, Mario and Sam.

To our friends old and new – we are so grateful to be on this rad journey that is life with you all. Fay. Jorja. Chandra. Sananda. Sandy. Kathryn. Louise. What wisdom and strength you share. Ruth, Mike and the rest of our magical Wagon Wheel bunch – how lucky we are. How inspiring you are. We love you.

Last – we have immeasurable gratitude for every person we've met along our journey, for all the good and the bad; it is all a gift. From the bottom of our hearts we thank you for touching our lives.

Shana Muldoon Zappa is a jewellery designer and writer who was born and raised in Los Angeles. With an endless imagination, a passion to inspire positivity through her many artistic endeavours, and her background in fashion, Shana created Star Darlings. She and her husband, Ahmet Zappa, collaborated on Star Darlings especially for their magical little girl and biggest inspiration, Halo Violetta Zappa.

Ahmet Zappa is the *New York Times* best-selling author of *Because I'm Your Dad* and *The Monstrous Memoirs of a Mighty McFearless*. He writes and produces films and television shows and loves pancakes, unicorns and making funny faces for Halo and Shana.

Leona's Unlucky Mission

Dear Mum and Dad,

First, star salutations for the care package! How did you know I needed a new toothlight? (Why are they so easy to lose?) And, Mum, your gamma-chip clusters are out of this world! I've already eaten half the box. They're soooooo starlicious I just can't stop! I know you said to share them with my roommate, Scarlet, and I would have, but guess what? She had to move out. Long story. (Don't worry, it wasn't my fault.) The good news is – you remember how she used to skateboard down the walls? Well, she won't be doing that anymore, at least not in my room! So for now I've got the whole room to myself – and it looks soooo much better without all that black!

I'm hoping to get a new roommate soon, though, and I'll let you know when I do. Stars crossed she's into a colour that goes a little bit better with gold – and that she's a lot more relaxed and not so hard to talk to.

Oh, and guess what! More big news! I formed a new band!!!!! It's called Star Darlings! And I'm the lead singer (of course)! We haven't played a gig yet, but I know we will, and I'll send you a holo-vid as soon as we do. We even have a manager, so it's the real deal! Remember Clover? Her colour is purple and she wears the hat? Anyway, her family is the Flying Molensas – as in the circus we used to go to every year! So she knows all about show business and she writes great songs. I know you keep saying that becoming a pop star is a moon shot, and that chances are a hydrong to one, but I have a starmendous feeling about us! And I might as well shoot for the stars, right? Isn't that what they're for?

Speaking of stars, I was looking at Grandpa's the other day, and I swear it winked at me!

Tell Felix congratulations on his promotion to assistant manager of the shoe shop. (I won't mention that Dad is his boss.) And tell Garfield I'll believe he has a girlfriend when he sends me a holo-pic. I'm waiting! (Ha-ha!)

Finally, tell Duchess and Francesca I'll holo-call them tonight if I have the chance. There's a first-year student here named Cassie who reminds me so much of Duchess, by the way. She has the same thick black lashes and soft rosy eyes. She's like a little doll you just want to pick up and hug!

I miss you and I love you.

Your superstar,

Leona

P.S. Send more clusters when you can!

Leona read over her holo-letter quickly, trying to think of what else to say. She tried to send one to her parents weekly, though sometimes she forgot. Sometimes, too, it was nearly impossible to write anything without giving her Star Darlings identity away. For instance, how could she explain Scarlet's moving out without mentioning that Scarlet had been dismissed from the group? She mailed her letter with a flick of her wrist. Hopefully, one day they'd all be able to share their secret with their families, but who knew when that would be?